By

Amanda Heartley

AMANDA HEARTLEY

Copyright and Disclaimer

This book is a work of fiction. The names, characters, places and incidents are products of the writer's imagination and have been used fictitiously and are not to be construed as real. Any resemblance to persons, living or dead, actual events, locales or organizations is entirely coincidental.

Copyright © 2017 Cheeky Books Ltd

Table of Contents

Coming soon, my next release!

If you want an email reminder about my next sinfully sexy story...

Sign up here!

http://join.amandaheartley.com

More from Amanda

Irresistible SEAL Box Set

A Military Romance

Runway Encounter Box Set

A South Beach Romance

Destiny Undone Series Collection

A Billionaire Romance

Fueled Obsession Box Set

A Bad Boy Romance

Oceans Apart Box Set

A British Billionaire Romance

Southern Heat Box Set

An Erotic Romance

Chapter One

Calvin

Goddammit! Every time I talked with that woman I fought with her. It was like we both came into the office with our dukes up. I tried to be nice on most occasions, but I was simply tired of the drama.

"For twelve years I've put up with your bullshit, Calvin," she fumed.

"In a few minutes you'll hardly ever see me again," I reminded her.

"After twelve years?" We'd fought this round before; she desperately wanted to control me.

"I'm out, Nadine, and there's nothing you can do about it." I was very proud of myself for staying calm.

"You've ruined me!" she exclaimed, always the pouting child.

"Sell your shares too, you hate the oil business, anyway," I coolly reminded her.

"You are a complete and total asshole!" Her eyes roved the room looking for something else to throw, but I'd packed up most of my breakable stuff and hauled it away already.

We were high school sweethearts, but I'd never let the fact that she was the richest girl in El Paso affect me. She was a gutsy little thing, and that was part of the reason why I fell in love with her. I remembered my eighteen-year-old self being awkward and sweaty when she asked me to dance. She was the most beautiful young woman I'd ever met, but she was spoiled, and I intended to spoil her more. I was a cowboy with a Stetson, dusty cowboy boots, and old school values. I grew up on the land

and didn't know much about dinner parties or idle chatter, but I wanted to carry a princess off into the sunset. Little did I know that she wasn't the right princess.

Shortly after our wedding, I saw that her boldness was just her being used to getting her own way. She soon lost interest in me and found relationships outside our marriage instead. Stupidly, we never discussed kids until after our wedding. I told her I wanted at least one, but it turned out she never wanted any.

Other differences cropped up during our marriage that pointed us firmly toward divorce and after five years, we ended things. Sadly, when her father, Harmon Flatfield, died, half of his company went to her and the other half to me. He never liked our getting divorced, so he married us to his company instead. She'd remarried twice after we went our separate ways. Even though she'd found other husbands to torture, she still really enjoyed taunting me—and her presence alone could do that. I was sure she showed up to work every day just so she could nag me, and I'd endured the situation for as long as I could.

Then one day, everything changed when I visited my grandfather's ranch. He'd died the previous year and left me the dilapidated old place. After listening to the long grass rustle in the breeze, the birds chirping in the wind, and breathing in the smell of earth and sky, I decided it was time to live my life differently. I was a rancher at heart. I grew up on the ranch, and I'd abandoned it all for a spoiled girl and the grind of the oil rigs that were destroying the very land I stood on.

I went back to work the next week, negotiated to sell my shares in the company to a competitor—which really pissed off my ex-wife—and I walked out with enough money to comfortably kiss my billionaire playboy lifestyle in the city goodbye, forever.

"You can't do this!" she threatened. "You can't just leave!"

"I can, darlin'... and I am so out of here." I winked and walked out. "See ya, Nadine."

I wanted to keep it simple, a clean break.

"Calvin!" she roared. "Fuck you!" I heard trailing behind me.

I was finally free. The sound of her crying filled the empty space between us, and for a moment I felt a bit of remorse—but not enough to turn around and go back.

***

That was a year ago, and I thought I'd have regrets, yet after all that time, I was still as much in love with the land, the sky, and the breeze as I'd ever been. I'd worked to rebuild the ranch, rejuvenated the alfalfa production, put my millions away in savings and tried to forget what money had done to me.

I was a solid man now. Lean from hard work, tanned from the Texas sun, and more focused on making a life that mattered than I'd ever been. Some say life on a ranch can be lonely, but it wasn't for me. I had people around me all the time though I didn't need anyone. I had the great purple sky and the wide-open spaces for company. My life was simple, quiet, and complete.

Little did I know, all that space was about to get much smaller as I watched the thirty-foot moving van pull up the dusty trail to Roanoke's ranch, a mile down the road. I knew Paul Roanoke was moving to Florida with his wife—they were getting older and wanted to be near their children—and there'd been a lot of gossip about who may have bought the old place.

The rumor of an elderly man and his young daughter was the one most often believed and my curiosity had spiked hearing that theory. A single woman about my age moving so close? She could be a dowdy old troll, or a daddy's girl, though—who knew.

It was more excitement than we usually got around here, and I was fascinated to find out. When I finally saw the new proprietors rumble down the road, I wanted to get a look for myself and as I watched the moving van kick up dust, I figured, I'd know soon enough.

Chapter Two

Lainey

On the long, hot, sunbaked drive from New York to Texas, I wasn't sure what was driving me crazier—the tedious hours in the car, or the fact that my dad had traded our posh New York City penthouse for a ranch in El Paso, Texas. *Who the hell does that?* I fumed.

We'd stopped speaking to each other a few miles back. I wasn't going to be the first one to give, and neither was he. With every mile we drove farther away from New York, it felt like another part of my soul got ripped away. I didn't want to live on a ranch in Texas and my only saving grace was that I'd planned to attend grad school at NYU in the fall. I only had to endure a summer on the ranch although my dad still tried to convince me to stay and make a life in Texas. I was sure he'd gone bat shit crazy.

I'd already put off grad school for a year while I created an elaborate bucket list for Mom who'd been diagnosed with stage four breast cancer when I was twenty. As soon as I got my BA, I made traveling to the Andes, hiking Mt. Fuji, and eating gelato on every continent with her, a life goal. My mom had a few goals of her own she wanted us to accomplish together, so we did.

I'd been so impressed that we'd ticked every item off her bucket list, that I hadn't seen the signs, and before I knew it, she was gone. Her dying wish was that Dad and I fill his bucket list together, but there was only one thing on it—buy a ranch in Texas.

Voila, we turned into the driveway of a mammoth-sized farmhouse in the middle of Nowhere, USA. I guess it's true what they say—

everything's bigger in Texas. I knew I was being a brat for hating it, but it wasn't on any of my lists anywhere... ever.

"Oh my God," was all I could choke out.

It was hard for him to hide his astonishment "It's much bigger than it seemed on the internet," he ogled.

"What are we going to do with all that space, Dad?" I asked, sounding lost.

"I know this isn't what you want, sweetheart," he confessed.

He looked sad and alone. I hadn't even really thought about Dad. I'd been too busy worrying about my own feelings, and my grief over losing my mother, I hadn't thought about him losing his wife. He hated Manhattan because it was everything she was. He was a country boy who'd fallen for a beautiful city girl thirty years earlier. The love story was legendary and yet, as I stared into his hazy blue eyes, I saw a man just as lost as I was.

"Who knows... I might fall in love with cows, and dirt, and..." I started to feel nauseous.

"You're too much like your mother, honey, but I appreciate you trying." I really loved my dad.

"It'll be a crazy adventure, that's for sure. Shall we go see the place?" I asked, hoping to change gears—I didn't need to cry anymore.

"I can't believe you bought a house without even flying out here to see it first," I playfully scolded.

"We Skyped a few times, and they showed me around. It looked perfect." He seemed to be doubting his own judgment at that moment.

"There isn't a family of cannibals waiting in the barn with chainsaws is there?" I asked, trying to lighten the mood.

"Oh, Lord. I hope not," Dad said, a bit rattled as he took a set of keys out of a FedEx envelope and fumbled with the ancient lock.

"Watch out for children with glaring white hair and vacant stares," I teased as he jimmied the wrong key into the hole.

As I terrorized my father, I saw a tractor in the distance and it seemed to be coming toward us, which got me worried. Maybe I'd freaked myself out watching old horror movies, but I was genuinely concerned as the tractor inched closer and closer to our house. I wanted to nudge my dad along, but thankfully he found the right key and the rusty door swung open on creaky hinges.

"Gonna have to oil that," I heard him mumble.

As soon as we entered, my heart fell a little deeper into my chest. It was massive, and not as dusty or decrepit as I thought it might have been, but it was tacky. Faded checked furniture, gauzy lace curtains, ancient hurricane lights. Kitsch, tack, and every kind of country-o-rama I could think of screamed out at me. Dated, old, backwoods, country—I wanted to throw up. And what was up with all the big stars everywhere, and all the stuff that said 'TEXAS' on it?

"Just needs a little paint here and there," Dad said with relief.

I rolled my eyes. "Dad, it needs a blowtorch. Why did you buy the place furnished?" I was being serious.

"Urban style isn't really chic in these parts. Good ol' country folk like things at a slower pace, more simple and timeless," he said.

"Ma and Pa Kettle. I get it, but isn't it too much, even for you, Dad?" He looked lost in thought, his eyes scanning the house as he walked toward the staircase. "Three days ago, you had taste," I muttered under my breath, then I heard a loud rumbling motor approach. "Shit... I mean... shoot, Dad!" I freaked.

He poked his head down from the stairway, cocking it slightly when he heard the loud rumbling come to a halt right at the door.

"Who do you think it is?" I asked, shaking.

"Probably just the neighbors," he scoffed, heading toward the door.

"Don't open it!" I screamed, frightening my father more than I should have.

"Oh, really, Lainey," he said as he answered the robust knock that followed.

When he opened the door, I nearly fell over. Standing before my father at around six and a half feet, and wearing a tall, dusty, cowboy hat was one of the most gorgeous men I'd ever seen. He looked a little weather-worn from being outside in the sun, yet had a face chiseled by the gods. I tried not to drool.

"Howdy," he said as he tipped his hat.

Really, we'd either fallen into the Twilight Zone or an alternate universe, because no one said "howdy". Not in real life? Did they?

"I'm Calvin Granger. I run the ranch on the north side of your property. I saw your moving van and wanted to come over for a quick hello." Oh, my God, he sounded like a gravel-voiced angel with a Texas drawl. I couldn't remember a man ever having this kind of visceral effect on me. I was like a giddy little school girl with butterflies in my stomach. All I thought about was envisioning his rough, stubbled face caressing my cheek. Oh my god, and what would that stubble feel like if it grazed across my nether region, I wondered?

"Hi, I'm Hal Campbell, and this is my daughter, Lainey," my dad responded cordially.

Don't sound dumb—get your game face on, Lainey.

"I'm Lainey." I rolled my eyes at myself. *Idiot.*

"Nice to meet you both," the dashing Calvin Granger replied. "We're having a BBQ tonight. It's going to be a beautiful evening, and I thought you two might want to join us after you've had some time to settle in. Most of the folks from around these parts will be there. It would be nice for you to get to know some of the locals." He seemed to be pitching us a reason to join him, as if he wasn't the most heavenly person on the planet already.

"We'd be glad to," my dad chimed in eagerly, almost too quickly—possibly believing he'd found the perfect reason to keep me here.

"Great! Starts around six-thirty. See you then," Calvin said, tipping his hat again.

Chapter Three

Calvin

I didn't know what drew me to the Roanoke Ranch that day. I guess I had to meet the new neighbors—my curiosity got the best of me since I'd heard they'd bought the place, sight unseen. An elderly man and his single daughter—the hero in me thought that neither seemed able to run such a large ranch on their own. They were city folk, and city folk were delicate.

I wasn't sure what I was expecting to find when I knocked on their door, but it definitely wasn't what I found. Lainey Campbell was absolutely one of the most stunning women I'd ever met. I thought my ex-wife was beautiful—once—but this woman was so well put together, from her perfectly windswept hair to the lavender toenail polish on her tanned feet.

Every curve of her body was so sexy. It had been a long time since my wife and I divorced and while I'd had a few women from time to time, but none had gripped me so immediately.

I still felt the same way when she walked through my door, looking like a Bohemian goddess. She was wearing a steel gray sundress that came to her mid-thigh and a necklace with an elaborate stone pendant. I had to bat away thoughts of kissing those shapely legs from her perfect toes, across the landscape of her well-toned thighs, and upward to heaven.

"Welcome y'all," I said as I ushered them in, still hazy with lust.

They'd brought expensive wine, and I stifled a good-hearted laugh. Wine wouldn't go over well with this beer-drinking crowd, but I appreciated it.

"Howdy," her father responded, and she rolled her eyes. I didn't think she intended to do it, but she did. I couldn't contain myself any longer and I laughed—kindly, I hoped.

"Thanks for inviting us," she added, trying to smooth over the edges.

"Glad you could join us," I replied.

God, I wanted to take her right then and there. I felt like I was possessed, which was insane because I didn't even know the woman. As the evening progressed, I was happy to see her father connect with a few of the other ranch hands and a few other friends I'd invited. He would need their help on the ranch and all of them were good people, willing to pitch in and work together.

Since her father was otherwise engaged, I got a moment to be alone with Lainey. I saw she'd made idle chit chat for some time with a throng of men who'd cornered her, like bees around a honey pot. The women, I noticed, stood by coolly and just watched, sizing her up and judging her, no doubt. It was going to be hard for her to fit in around here, but my heart swelled for her. Seeing her glass was nearly empty, I popped the cork on a fresh bottle of wine, and seized my opportunity to interrupt the parade of suitors.

"Are you enjoying the BBQ?" I asked as I approached.

Her beautiful, wide smile was captivating.

"I am," she said with strain.

I chuckled, realizing she clearly wasn't, and raised the bottle of wine. It was an excellent Pinot Noir I'd saved for this moment. She recognized the winery it had come from and her face brightened some.

"May I fill your glass? I noticed you were getting low." Finally, she gave me a genuine smile.

"Yes, please." She seemed relieved and raised her glass toward me.

"To the rescue," I said, tipping the bottle, and her eyes told me she understood my double meaning as I poured the wine.

"Thank you," she sighed.

"You bet." That small exchange of words was enough to know I wanted to be alone with her. Very alone.

Half the men who'd been ogling Lainey were married, and the other half had girls who thought they were in relationships with them. Only one truly single rival was any threat, and I was determined to knock him across the playing field and out of the park, but first, I had to get rid of the married men.

"Hey, Ralph, where's Mary? I haven't seen her for a while." Of course, I knew exactly where Mary was. She and Tom's wife, Abigail, had gone upstairs to put their toddlers to bed for the night.

Ralph's face reddened, as did Tom's, being caught red-handed flirting with the new girl.

"They went to put the kids down," Ralph mumbled. "Guess we should go check in with them. Nice meeting you, Lainey," he said as they sheepishly retreated.

Lainey's eyes perked up. Boy, I liked her even more the way she flashed those baby blues at me.

"Thanks for your advice on the farm equipment," she said as they slowly moved away. I knew she was trying to sound sincere, but the statement came off as absurd. "I'll let you know what my dad and I decide."

"Sure thing," Ralph replied over his shoulder as he slunk away.

That was the call to scatter, and everyone— even my lone rival—returned to the BBQ to find their spouses or girlfriends, leaving Lainey and I together.

"Sorry about that, I hope they didn't bore you too much, but they don't see too many new faces around here," I apologized.

"Oh, it wasn't that bad, though I was beginning to feel like Scarlet O'Hara at Twelve Oaks." She laughed, hoping I'd get the reference. "It's okay, they meant well," she said with a smile—and she had such an amazing smile, too.

"Do you want to take a walk, or would you like some more food?" I offered. What I really wanted to do was whisk her away from everything and everyone, but I was a gentleman and the choice was hers to make.

AMANDA HEARTLEY

"A walk sounds nice." Bingo, a lightning flash of nerves shivered my spine and rocketed straight to my cock. I slowly reeled her in as we walked together. I showed her my horses and the barn animals. It was obvious she was way outside of her comfort zone, but she was being gracious about everything, then she innocently asked me a question that had me in stitches.

"So, do you still call yourselves cowboys? Or are you cow people now? How does the cow... modifier work in these days of political correctness?"

She was being earnest, but came off sounding completely weird. I knew she must have had a vision of banjos, whoopin' and hollerin', and shit-kickin' in her head, and I wanted to tell her that modern cowboys were honest men of the land and weren't gun-toting land jockeys fighting Indians anymore. She'd understand our way of life soon enough, though—no need to start defending my existence just yet. I was sure when she met my best friend, Alan Redfeather, her ideas about Old West Cowboys and Indians would fade.

We stopped at the gazebo I'd built between my house and the alfalfa fields. It was a place I liked to go to when I wanted to get away from everything. I could see the cows and sheep from that spot and the alfalfa fields in the distance. At this vantage point, I could survey the entire expanse of my property. We sat there for a while, just talking, and got to know one another better.

"I bet New York never seemed so far away," I started.

Her head dropped, and I wondered if I'd upset her.

"You have no idea," she said softly, rubbing her fingers.

"Downtown El Paso is only about half an hour from here and we have some of the best Mexican restaurants in the world. It's not New York, but if you ever want to run away to Mexico for the weekend, it's just a hop over the border." I was selling, I knew, but I didn't want her starting her life here hating my hometown.

"Thanks. I'm sure it's exciting. It's just that I miss the noise, the bustle... and the people. We've only been here a few hours, but I feel like I'm living in another country." She crinkled her nose in a way that made her look immature, yet so adorable.

"It's not too exciting here compared to the city. I understand." I smiled and patted her on the back. I wasn't ready to let her know that I'd lived a life like hers in New York with endless meetings, an insane schedule, and people, lots of people... everywhere. I wanted her to fall in love with everything she saw first before I'd let her in on that part of my life.

"In fact," I added, "You're probably the most exciting thing to come around these parts in a long time," I said, and smiled at her in what I hoped was a seductive way.

She laughed and shook her head.

"Is that the best you've got, cowboy?" she playfully reprimanded.

"Sadly, yes," I laughed. "I'm a little out of practice," I confessed, genuinely embarrassed.

Her piercing eyes met mine, and she shot me a hot, smoldering glare. I'd forgotten how much I loved modern women.

AMANDA HEARTLEY

Chapter Four

Lainey

While I really didn't want to like it in Texas, somehow Calvin made me feel more at home with each passing minute. We talked for a few hours the first night I arrived, his deep Texan accent giving me goosebumps whenever he spoke, and by the time people started to filter out from the barbecue, Calvin and I were practically making out like teenagers.

We were naughty, sneaking away from a gathering he was hosting, and yet, it seemed to continue just fine without him. The guests sat around talking, eating food, drinking beer, and occasionally hollering over to us sitting in the darkness to check we were okay. Our absence from the main party didn't seem to cause alarm and as it got later, everyone drifted over one-by-one to say their goodbyes and thank Calvin for the evening.

"You two seem to be getting along pretty good," Dad said as he approached us in the gazebo and Calvin stood to face him. "I've had a great time, but I'm heading home now. Are you coming, Lainey?"

"Not yet. I'll be home in a little while. Just getting to know our neighbor here," I replied.

"Well, all right. Just don't be stopping up all night. We've got everything to unpack tomorrow," he said in a tone that let me know he wasn't fooled about what was going on. I could've died of embarrassment right there and I felt my cheeks burning. I was just thankful it was dark, so no one could see.

"I won't, Dad. I'll just finish this rather large glass of wine then I'll be coming home, I promise."

"Okay. Well, you kids be good and thanks for inviting us over, Calvin," Dad said, shaking his hand.

"Real neighborly of you to welcome us like that and I hope we can return the favor sometime."

"It was a pleasure, sir. Been nice meeting you both and if you need any help with anything, please just ask."

"Oh, I'm sure you're gonna regret making that offer," Dad chuckled as he turned to leave. "See you soon."

I could've talked to Calvin all night, but inside I was dying to kiss that stubbled face. I felt wanton and needy, and I didn't care how bold I was—I wanted to ride that cowboy. After he'd confessed to being out of practice when it came to the subtleties of dating, I thought, dating be damned, I just wanted a kiss, so I gently grabbed his face and planted a soft peck on his tender mouth.

I was expecting rugged leather, but his lips were smooth and gentle, and when he returned my kiss, I opened my mouth and let him in. He felt warm and comfortable as his soft tongue slipped in deeper, caressing mine with gentle strokes. I ran my fingers through his hair, grabbing a handful of it and tenderly tugging. I needed him closer, deeper. I felt so horny. I wanted his body and soul. He responded to my advances and shifted closer to me. My aching nipples pressed against the thin material of my sundress, and I was glad I wasn't wearing a bra. I had small, perky breasts, so they didn't need one, anyway.

I couldn't believe how forward I was being. In truth, it had been a long time since I'd dated, too. After spending a year traveling with my mom, and another year grieving over her death, I'd had neither the time, nor the inclination for men. I felt so willful kissing my hot neighbor before even one of my bags were unpacked, and I'd probably have some explaining to do in the morning, but right then, there on that bench under the wide-open midnight sky, it felt so right.

As I pressed my chest into his, he withdrew from my mouth for a moment and whispered in my ear in his sexy-as-hell Southern drawl as his hand gently hovered near my beckoning breasts.

"I want you, Lainey."

I almost melted into a puddle when he gently nibbled my earlobe, his hand cupping my breast. "I want you, too," I sighed, softly nestling his calloused hand into my sundress.

"You are beautiful," he said as he tenderly slipped a strap from my shoulder, exposing my pert and wanton nipples to the moonlight and his steamy gaze.

His hand grazed over the aching bud and I could feel the roughness of his skin as he teased it even tauter, striking a fire between my legs that made me writhe with desire. He chuckled at my reaction which made me laugh, too.

"I'm not normally this forward, but I feel like a horny teenager with an insane crush right now," I confessed.

"Me too," he said as his thumb danced across my breast again.

A hot sigh escaped me, and that was his cue to lower his lips to my aching nipple and devour it, softly. I felt his scruff tickle my skin—a heady mix of startling sensations and pure pleasure. I bucked against him, my thigh rubbing his erection—thick and solid. He moved me closer, lifting me in his strong arms and shifting me into his lap. I sat astride his rock-hard cock and presented my other, neglected, nipple to his mouth. I slowly rocked on him, feeling his length strengthening under my soaking wet panties.

He grabbed my ass with both hands as he continued to nibble and tug on my nipples with his teeth. First one, then the other. Pulling me in closer to him as I continued to rock back and forth, stimulating his erection nestling between my legs. I couldn't help letting out a moan—I wanted more.

Suddenly, he stopped his exquisite ministrations on my breasts, leaving me ravenous with desire.

"I, um... I..." he stuttered.

I looked down at him, confused. I knew it was late, like long past midnight, and my dad... well, that could be an awkward breakfast conversation, but I was twenty-three for God's sake. It wasn't like I was a virgin.

"What's wrong?" I asked, concerned.

"Um, this is kinda awkward for me to say. Don't get me wrong, I think you're a beautiful gal and all, but..."

"But, what? You're not one of those Brokeback Mountain cowboys are ya?" I interrupted. *After all this time without a man, please don't tell me I've hit on a gay boy*, I thought, pulling up my dress to cover my exposed breasts.

"No!" he half-shouted, shaking his head. "I mean, no I'm not," he reiterated in a quieter tone. "I really want to make out with you. Right now, right here, but I... you... we just met a few hours ago, and you're my new neighbor and all. I like to think I'm a gentleman, so we should probably stop this before we do something we might regret in the morning, you know?"

He was doing a great job of taming his passions, but I saw the wild look in his eye and I felt his arousal between my legs.

"Calvin, we're grown-ups. We can do crazy things," I said as I pressed myself onto his cock, wanting it inside me. "Are you worried I'll get all possessive, just because we had sex the first day we met?"

"No, I'm worried you'll think I'm a total asshole." He seemed so earnest in what he said.

I lifted myself off him and watched as his face dropped.

"It's probably for the best," he said, in an attempt to console himself. "I don't know what came over me. I should have had more control, but I really like you."

"I know what came over you," I smiled as I slipped out of my soaked panties and tossed them in his lap. "Because it came over me too." I leaned in and kissed him sweetly on his gorgeous lips. "But maybe you're right. Maybe we're moving too fast, and this isn't normally me at all. I'm usually far more of a lady than to give myself to a man I've only known for a couple hours."

He brushed the hair away from my face, the tips of his fingers gently trailing down my cheek. "I'm sure you are," he said, then he looked back at my panties, all crumpled on the bulge in his jeans and scooped them up in his huge hand.

"Whatchoo gonna do with those, cowboy?" I asked, and stood there shocked when, without saying a word, he lifted them to his nose and took a long, deep breath—like he was inhaling a drug. Watching him do that?

So.

Fucking.

Hot.

"I can't believe you just did that. No one's ever done that with my panties before. Is this a Texan thing? Are y'all crazy out here?" I said, but it had turned me on even more as I felt the cool night air on my wet pussy.

"I'd be crazy if I didn't. I bet you taste as good, as well," he said, tucking my discarded underwear into the pocket of his jeans.

"Seriously? You're keeping my panties, dude?" I said with a smile.

"Yep. You don't mind, do you? Just a little memento from our wonderful time together tonight."

"Uh... um... I guess not, but I'd better be unpacking fast tomorrow. They were my last spare pair I put on for the BBQ," I said incredulously. He just gave me a big smile then took my hand.

We laid together beneath the night sky, just talking and getting to know each other a little more. He felt good nestled against me. I didn't want to move, even though I was desperate for a shower with the muggy Texas heat clinging to my skin, and the grass and dirt laced in my hair. I had to be home before sunrise—I didn't want my dad even thinking we'd been doing anything but talking all night.

"I should probably get home... before my dad worries," I suggested.

He lifted his head and smiled.

"If you must," he fake-pouted.

"It's not like he'd really be bothered. He's a totally cool father, and I can tell he likes you, but it is our first night here," I laughed.

"Well, I'm glad we met and had some time together," he said, trailing his finger across my wrist then bringing it to his mouth and kissing it.

"I am, too," I smiled as I gently caught his hand in mine. I'd enjoyed our crazy night, but it was time to get cleaned up, get some rest, and figure out what I was going to do with my life. I looked over at Calvin. He seemed as unsure of his next move as I did, so I took the lead. After all, it was my reputation in a new town I had to consider.

I bent in and kissed him softly on the lips then tightened my arms around my chest. I looked down to check myself and swiped as much of the dirt from my dress as I could to make myself look somewhat presentable.

"I don't have your number, or I'd say I'll call you... or um something." God, I was feeling awkward. He seemed to understand my embarrassment and was smooth and confident in his reply.

"Go home and get some sleep. I'll come by tomorrow afternoon to take you and your dad into

AMANDA HEARTLEY

town. I'm sure you'll need groceries and other essentials. A moving truck probably isn't the easiest of vehicles to park at the store."

"I completely forgot, we don't even have a car," I replied. "We didn't need one in New York City. There was no point as we had a driver if we needed one." I knew that sounded pretentious as soon as I'd said it. We didn't have our own driver—we hired one, but it was too late at night to worry about details like that.

"Well, maybe we can find you a reliable vehicle while we're in town, as well." He was nothing but charm itself.

"You really want to see me again after our little awkward moment?" I asked. I knew I could run, but where would I hide, anyway?

"Of course, Lainey... and the sooner the better," he said earnestly.

"See you tomorrow then," I said as I sauntered off, not knowing, nor wanting to know what time it was. He watched me walk down the road to our ranch, and after glancing over my shoulder a few times and waving, I realized he was going to carry on standing there and watching me until I got into our new house safely. Such a gentleman.

I snuck into the house, grateful that my dad wasn't sitting up waiting for me. I'd only spent a few hours in the place before we left for the BBQ and I couldn't even remember where my room was. I knew it was upstairs somewhere, but I wasn't in the mood to go peering around a dark, scary house by myself.

Even though I was grown and knew that there was no way a boogie man or a clown would jump out and get me, I was mildly afraid something would. I was so far out of my element away from NYC, my instincts were shot. I found the downstairs bathroom and took the fastest shower in recorded history, the scene in Psycho playing on my mind as I scrubbed and washed my body. When I was done, I grabbed a big, fluffy dressing gown out of my suitcase in the lounge and headed for the god-awful couch to get a little shut-eye until morning, unconsciously preparing myself to face my dad.

Chapter Five

Calvin

I walked home and was totally surprised to find a few hang-arounds from the BBQ and an Armageddon-sized mess to deal with the following morning. I thought everyone had left, but those sitting by the dwindling bonfire were completely drunk and almost incoherent. Instead of kicking them all out, which was what I really wanted to do, I decided a little diversion would be a fun way to wind down the evening.

I was walking in a haze of love or more likely, lust. I couldn't accurately pin my emotions, but they were raw and right at the surface. I just wanted to enjoy that intoxication that no liquor on earth could provide. Only Lainey, and everything she was, seemed to have the power to alter me so greatly and I'd only just met her. Was it infatuation?

Honestly, I needed a drink and a little levity to pull me out of my fog. Left waxing philosophically, clutching a Lonestar, and spouting off about field turnover, Ed had dominated the conversation for most of the evening. I loved my neighbors, but wow, their conversation, while passionate, was often amazingly dull. Of course, that all changed when I walked up to them.

"Well, lookee here what the cat dragged in," a very inebriated Lindsay Triton said, looking at me a little more seductively than I was expecting.

Lindsay was my farthest neighbor on the east side. She was a widow with two grown sons and usually her conversation was tame. But after guzzling a few beers and some of Vernon Pillar's homemade whiskey—which could turn your insides into molten lava—she became quite enamored with everyone and everything.

"Whatcha been doing out there in that gazebo of yours?" she interrogated. "Can't be anything godly," she said with a chuckle, and I laughed at her remarkably accurate insinuation.

"I was getting to know my new neighbor, Lainey, and we lost track of time. She's a city girl, so it's going to take a while for her to adjust here, I fear." I was being sincere and hoping that sincerity would throw the bloodhound off the trail.

"Getting to know her, huh? I ain't blind nor stupid, son. I see you two young'uns canoodling over there," she said with a knowing grin.

"Canoodling? Who still says that?" I laughed. "But, anyway, we were just talking, and I told her just how nice all my neighbors were. You are nice, aren't you, Lindsay?" I teased, and she let out a grunt of disdain and rolled her eyes at me.

"You should know that city folks get eaten up and spat out with the seeds around here," she said as she spat on the ground for effect.

"I don't give 'em more than a year," Vernon chimed in, slurring his words.

"That girl's far too pretty for these parts," Lyndsay continued. "Men around here need a solid woman by their side," she said as she raised her hands to her huge, sagging breasts, adjusting them more tightly into her V-neck t-shirt, then nonchalantly pointed them in my direction. Anyone could see that shirt was at least one size too small to house those mighty bazookas, if not two, and I immediately raised my hands in surrender. "Don't shoot, Lindsay. I give up," I joked, and everyone laughed out loud. She looked a little indignant, but soon enough a big smile spread across her face when she saw the funny side.

"In your dreams, Calvin," she replied. "You ain't man enough to handle these puppies," she said, crossing her arms across her chest and suddenly, the laughter was turned on me.

For a moment, I wondered why I'd ever befriended these people. They were simple folk who'd never strayed far from their land. They had no idea what New York was like and to them, it might as well have been as far away as the moon. They'd only ever orbited in their small world, and some had never even been out of their own state.

As kings and queens of their crops and pastures—they could be rather arrogant, opinionated, yet entirely fascinating at the same time. If I was honest though, people in big business— especially the oil business—were no less arrogant or full of their own self-importance, but perhaps they were better at hiding it.

My immediate goal, however, was to dispel any rumors or impressions that Lainey and I were doing anything other than just talking—that's all we did, after all. She said she was a lady, and I had no reason to doubt her. As a proper gentleman, I shouldn't have assumed she'd be willing to have sex with me on the very day we met. However, once opinions were formed, these country folks would relentlessly grind the gossip mill, and I was sure Lainey would never survive the scandal of it if they did.

I hung out with the remaining guests for a little longer, talking about ranching, reliving times we'd spent together and anything else I could think of to take the focus off me and Lainey to deter them from gossiping about us. Eventually, the conversation subsided, and I mentioned that it was past two in the morning and it was time for me to head off to bed.

I did offer for them to stay as long as they wanted, but it seemed to have the desired effect, and everyone got up and ambled home. I suppose I should've cleaned up the place a little as my regular cleaner was on vacation, but frankly, I was exhausted. It could wait until the morning and I headed off to bed, excited about the prospect of seeing Lainey again the next day.

I usually woke at seven, no matter how late I stayed up the night before, but I was shocked to discover I'd slept until ten; I hadn't done that since I was a teenager. I still felt groggy and fog-headed, so I stumbled to the kitchen to make a pot of strong coffee.

I didn't even want to look at the mess I knew was waiting for me on the porch and the side yard until I'd taken a good, healthy swig of Joe. In fact, I was on my second cup when I glanced through the window and noticed everything outside had already been cleaned up. My mind felt a blaze of bewilderment. Who had cleaned my house? Did the cleaner come back early, or did I get her vacation dates wrong?

Not many of my neighbors were the do-gooder type. They be there in a heartbeat to help each other when someone was in need, but never just show kindness unless it was some sort of tragedy. I walked out onto my porch to find Lindsay sitting on the porch swing, taking in the view. I was a little disappointed to discover who my mystery maid was since I secretly hoped it had been Lainey who'd come over.

Not that I wanted her to clean up for me exactly, but knowing she was here and doing something nice would have been exciting. I had such an infatuation with her, but I knew I had to keep my thoughts under control. As I thought of Lainey, my cock started to stiffen, and I sure didn't want Lindsay getting the wrong impression.

"Morning," I chirped jovially as I took a seat in the chair across from her. "Did you clean up my yard?" I asked, trying to sound appreciative.

"Me? Clean up your shit? Nah, I came over to get more dirt on that girl. I must have been so drunk last night, I forgot everything you said." She leaned in as if she was expecting me to give her some juicy gossip.

My mind did a mental eye roll. "She's a nice girl," was all I said.

"Nice to look at maybe, but she ain't Texan," Lindsay said with a note of disgust.

"I'm not much for gossiping this morning, Lindsay. We just talked as I said last night. Is there something else I can help you with? Do you want some coffee?" I was suddenly irritated with her intrusion and her attempt to put Lainey down as an outsider.

"So, you aren't gonna throw me a bone, huh?" she pushed.

"There are no bones to throw. We shared a bottle of wine and had a nice chat," I told her plainly.

"Okay, okay. I get it. Maybe she is nice, we'll see." She seemed pacified for the moment then said, "The faucet on my sink is busted." She smiled a big smile, showing off all her crooked and decaying teeth. "I thought you might be a doll..." She didn't have to finish.

"Give me a few minutes to freshen up and I'll be over," I responded, not terribly enthused by the task ahead of me.

I figured I'd either help Lindsay or she'd be in my hair all day, and if Lainey was feeling anything like I felt, she probably needed a few more hours of sleep before I went back over there. However, the prospect of calling on her was enough motivation for me to get moving.

"Do you mind hanging out here while I get ready?" I asked, not really wanting her milling around my place.

"Sure... unless you want me to come scrub your back... or anything else?" she said with a grin.

"Um, thanks for the offer, but I'm a big boy now. I think I'll be fine on my own," I said, my face burning with embarrassment.

"I'll bet you are," she muttered, her eyes tracing down my body to my crotch and lingering there.

I smiled nervously, and my hands moved unconsciously to block her gaze. "Uh... right. I'll be back as quick as I can," I said, and turned abruptly to go back into the house.

I felt annoyed as I walked toward the bathroom. She could have just called instead of coming over unannounced. At least if she'd called, I would've been spared starting off my morning with an unwelcome view of her one-piece, strapless, and short jumpsuit—which was her signature two sizes too small, of course.

That hideous outfit was so tiny, her butt cheeks were barely contained within it, leaving me with nothing to wonder about what was inside. Nope, not interested... at all. I took a quick shower, threw on an old pair of jeans and T-shirt, and went out to greet her again.

"Mmm, mmm, mmm," she exclaimed, hungrily. If only I had a gorilla suit to wear instead.

"Okay, I'll have to make this a quick trip, Lindsay. I have a lot to get done today," I warned.

"It's Saturday, whatcha gotta do?" she pried.

"A lot of stuff," is all I gave her.

"Okay, let's take my truck. I promise to have you back before you turn into a pumpkin," she laughed, thinking herself riotously funny. I'd been driven to her place in her truck a hundred times before, so I couldn't really protest this time—but I wanted to. The last thing I wanted to do was be at the mercy of this woman.

AMANDA HEARTLEY

60

Chapter Six

Lainey

I had trouble sleeping, so when I heard my father stirring, I woke to face whatever music there might be.

"Morning, Dad," I said, sounding more chipper than I felt.

"Morning, kiddo. You sleep ok?"

Great, Dad was chipper too. No trouble yet.

"Oh, not bad for our first night here. I'm sure we'll settle in soon. Calvin offered to take us into town later, by the way. I think all we have left for breakfast from the road trip are the Nescafe packets and some granola bars." I tried not to, but it sounded like I was making a peace offering.

Come on, Lainey, buck up. You're a grown woman, you can talk to strangers, or um... neighbors you hardly know if you want. Boy did I feel weird.

"Granola bars sound good to me," he said kindly. "That Calvin is a nice man, isn't he? I'm glad you two hit it off as well as you did last night." He smiled and moved to look for a kettle in an opened moving box.

Wow, that might have been it.

No lecture, no *"Honey, I'm just looking out for your best interests."* Maybe that was the end of it. Whew, perhaps he did recognize that I wasn't a child anymore. Despite avoiding a Dad lecture, I was still nervous—something just felt off. It was probably the fact that I resisted the move and I was still in shock that we were actually in Texas. Strangely, all I wanted to do was run to see Calvin again. Somehow, being with him made it all better.

Dad and I finished the breakfast, which really didn't satisfy us, but it was all we had unless we wanted to drive the moving van into town. We didn't have to return the U-Haul for another two days, so I suggested we keep it so we could buy furniture. I planned to set the garish, powder puff pink bedroom set in my room on fire, so there was that to replace, at least.

I hoped to convince my dad to dump it all, but I didn't want to push my luck. We also needed to buy a car and a truck, so we had quite a bit of shopping to do. Hopefully, there were decent grocery stores in town since I was craving brie and a baguette, but I didn't want to get my heart set on anything. Maybe that's why I was so into Calvin. He seemed real, and somehow, familiar.

"What time did he say we would head into town?" Dad asked.

I think he was ready to settle in and get his life in Texas started. Me, I was dragging my feet. I looked at the clock, and it was only seven in the morning. Wow, no wonder I felt so funky. I'd only had about five hours sleep. I looked through the window over to Calvin's place and while it was hard to see in the distance, it looked a wreck from the BBQ party.

"I don't know. He didn't say, but it looks like a tornado has swept through his place over there. He'll probably need some help cleaning up first, I'd think."

"Good. That'll give me some time to figure out all the fix-its we need around here. I want to make sure we get the right supplies." Dad was giddy, like a kid in a candy store.

"Oh my god, you are such a dad!" I scolded.

"Yep, gotta be me," he claimed.

"I'm going to head back over to Calvin's and see if I can help him clean up." I thought Dad would easily sniff out my plan, but he didn't let on if he had. He seemed lost in his own little world of making lists of stuff to buy as he checked the place over.

"Sure, honey. I'll see you in a few. Tell him thanks again for inviting us over last night." He was such a cute, sincere old man, and I felt lucky to have him.

When I got to Calvin's, the house was completely quiet. It seemed like he was still sleeping, which struck me as odd because I thought cowboys always got up with the sun. I didn't want to wake him if he was still in bed, so I found the trash bins around the side of the barn and tidied up his yard and porch. It looked a lot, but it didn't take me that long before the place was all cleaned up and I was in desperate need of another shower.

I checked one more time to see if Prince Charming was awake yet, but it was all still very quiet inside. Then an icy chill ran down my spine—maybe he was hiding from me? *Oh, come on, Lainey,* I chastised myself. I wasn't insecure, it's just, well, the whole 'my name is Lainey, I'm a dainty lady' thing still had me twisted in knots.

As I got out of the shower in the second story bathroom, I saw Calvin on his porch with one of the women from the previous night. It was hard to tell from that vantage point, but they seemed to be having fun. I heard her laughing then they then got into her truck and drove away. I didn't want to feel jealous and angry, but I couldn't help it—I felt so... used.

There I was the night before, beating myself up for having a fling with a man I'd just met, and the very next morning he was off with someone else. I knew it wasn't like we were boyfriend and girlfriend, and I did tell him I wasn't going to get all possessive over him, but wasn't he the one who said he didn't want to look like an asshole? I guess he was proud of himself for waiting a few hours before he hooked up with someone else.

I knew how crazy I was sounding, but I couldn't stop myself from going there.

Chapter Seven

Calvin

The faucet repair was taking forever, which I knew was intentional on her part. First, she couldn't find her tools. Then she had to take all the stuff out from underneath her sink. Then I needed a flashlight that she couldn't seem to locate. The kicker was when she smoothed her hand over my ass as I bent over her sink, trying to get the rusted pipe loose.

Her advances didn't stop there, either. She bent down and pressed her massive chest onto my arm, claiming to see what the trouble was. The worst was when I finished the repair and crawled under the sink to turn the water on. She reached through my legs from behind me and grabbed my dick, hard. I jerked my head up in surprise and banged it on the sink.

"And what about this faucet?" she asked, all breathy as she feverishly fondled and stroked my manhood.

What the fuck?

"That faucet is mine, Lindsay, and it's working just fine. It doesn't need any help," I said, batting her hand away.

"It doesn't even need a little inspiration?" she asked, stroking me again even harder.

"For Christ's sake, Lindsay! It's time for me to go home." I was serious and hoped I sounded that way.

"Just bend me over the couch then, I'll take it quick and dirty," she pleaded, unzipping her jumpsuit and revealing her breasts.

"What the hell has gotten into you?" Now I was livid.

She looked me square in the eye.

"I saw you last night. I watched for quite a while, and you two weren't just talking. It's been a helluva long time for me, so if you're doling out the dick, I'm ready for my slice. If you don't give me some of that," she threatened as she stared at my semi-aroused cock, "I'm sure the rest of the folks would be eager to know all about the ho who just moved into town."

"You wouldn't!" I glared at her. "And she's no ho. You don't even know her," I defended.

She continued to undress. "I already got wet watching you under my sink, so I'm ready for it, baby," she said as she moved in on me. "Now, give it to me... hard and fast... or I'll make sure your little girlfriend's name will be mud around here."

"No!" I yelled. "First, don't even think about threatening me or Lainey... ever. Secondly, your

behavior is deplorable. Begging for sex. Is that
something your sons would be proud of? Their
mother no better than a two-bit whore?"

I was out of my mind with rage. "Take me
home. Now. And if you say a word to try to drag my
name through the mud... or Lainey's... I promise,
everyone will know what happened here. You lured
me here and forced your unwelcome attention on me.
Let's see whose word they'll believe. Yours, or mine?
I am so out of here."

I walked toward the door when she grabbed
my arm and stopped me.

"I'm sorry, Calvin... I... it's just... it's been so
darn long since I've been with a man and none of
them around here are even half the man you are." She
seemed genuinely sorry and ashamed as she covered
herself up again and zipped up her jump suit.

"That's not my problem. Ok, so you're horny, but you can't go around molesting whoever you feel like. If I did that to a woman, I'd be in jail right now. We aren't in the dark ages. You don't need to go to a barn raising to find a man. Just get online and start clicking, or swiping, or whatever works for you," I said as I started to calm down.

"You're right. I should never have done what I did. My hormones just got the better of me," she replied, hanging her head.

"I'm sure you're a very loving woman, but just so we're clear, and in the kindest way I can say this, I'm not interested in anything other than a friendship with you. And after this, I'm not even sure about that. My feelings are not gonna change." I wasn't exactly shocked by her indecent proposal, just disappointed because I had considered her a friend.

I truly understood her problem, and she was right, there weren't many available men around, but that wasn't my fault. I wondered why Lindsay had ramped up the volume now. She'd always been flirtatious, if not a little overtly, but nothing to this degree. I looked her in the eye.

"I care about you, okay? Just not in a romantic way." I think she finally got it, because she grabbed her keys, and we headed for her truck. I felt a wave of relief.

When we got back to my place, I gave her a hug and a peck on the cheek to show there were no hard feelings on my side. As soon as she pulled out of the drive, I looked over to Lainey's place. It was about noon, so I figured now would be a good time to call on her.

Chapter Eight

Lainey

I wouldn't say I was stalking him exactly, but in reality, I was—ravenously. I couldn't take my eyes off his place. I convinced myself I had a legitimate reason though. Dad and I were starving and there was no way I was going to bust into the last of the saltine crackers that sat cracked and soggy at the bottom of our road trip snack bag.

Instead, I sat with bated breath until I saw him return. Even though he'd come back in her truck, neither of them seemed to show any emotion. She stayed in her truck as he got out and he went straight to his own truck. I watched him drive over and within a moment he was on our front step. My stomach bloomed with butterflies, my mouth went dry, and I literally thought I was going to have a heart attack.

Crap, I had it bad. Luckily, my dad answered the door.

I wanted to be angry with him and give him the cold shoulder for going off with someone else that morning, but I kept reminding myself that I didn't have the right to do that. He didn't owe me anything, and we committed to nothing the previous night. Life could resume as usual.

"Lainey, we're going. Come on down," Dad hollered.

"Yep," was the only word I could muster.

I came downstairs wearing a breezy blouse that was sheer enough to show there was a pair of beautiful breasts beneath it, but also substantial enough not to be a peep show. He took notice. I had on my favorite pair of jeans as well. If I was going to feel lost and vulnerable, I wanted to at least be wearing clothes that gave me super powers—if only in my head.

"Don't you look lovely," Calvin noted with his sexy Southern accent.

I wasn't going to let myself be wooed. He probably said that to all the girls. Those Southern boys and their charm.

"Thank you," somehow made its way out of my mouth.

He gave me a weird look.

I was busted.

"Shall we go? I bet you're starving," he said with a lilt in his voice.

"I know I sure am," Dad piped in.

"Yep, I could eat a horse... I mean, not a horse, you guys don't... eat them, right? I mean, I don't." *Oh,*

Lainey, shut up! Just keep your mouth quiet for the rest of the day.

Calvin laughed. "Not usually. I know a great Mexican restaurant though. I thought we'd have some Carne Asada and cerveza," he offered.

"I actually know what that is, Mr. Fancy talker." *Lainey! What did I say about talking?* I chided myself.

My dad looked a little bewildered. "Anything sounds good to me," he added, then Calvin led us to his truck, and we headed toward town.

The food we had for lunch was amazing. We had some great Mexican spots in New York, but this was the real deal, and everything was fresh, spicy, and tasty. Calvin and my dad talked cars most of the time and they went off to look at some while I hit the grocery store. It wasn't as bad as I thought it would be, and I found a nice wedge of brie. Sadly, no baguettes, but I did discover a bakery with some artisan bread that smelled delicious. I also found a few wines I recognized and deli items I needed. All in all, my shopping was okay, but I would be on the hunt for a better grocery store soon. It was so far away from what I was used to in New York.

When we met up again, and I told Calvin, he laughed at me. He said the town was roaring with excitement and that was the best grocery store they'd seen in twenty years, and in three times as many miles. My heart sunk a little, but at least he'd helped my dad buy a used pickup, and a lightly used sedan for longer trips.

While I was happy to be settling in, it also created a feeling of dread. Did I really want to be putting down roots here among all the dust and dirt? However, I was glad there was a decent-ish grocery store, and we were now mobile. I guessed my pretty, pink powder-puff bedroom would have to wait as I couldn't order the items I liked online as the stores wouldn't deliver to our locale. The only decent furniture store was in downtown El Paso, so our day of excitement was over and we went back to the ranch.

Luckily, my dad didn't need to make any money. He had his retirement, and huge savings from the sale of the penthouse. We didn't need income from the ranch, but he wanted to work on the land, anyway. Calvin offered to come over and help him on how to best use the place another day. He looked tired, and I was sure he was ready for a cup of tea and some ESPN; luckily the cable was being installed when we returned.

"Thanks for all of your help, Calvin," he said. "I'm not sure how I would have managed without you. The two of you probably want some time to yourselves, so I'll just go tuck myself away and see what's on the television," he said as he made his exit.

"He's a bit old school," I said with a laugh. My dad was just such a typical father when it came to TV with his sports and 24-hour news.

"I really like him. He's a great guy. So, do you have plans tonight?" Calvin asked cautiously.

I'd totally forgotten about my jealousy over the woman I'd seen him with that morning, but his invitation brought it all back to me, so I played the snarky card.

"No, do you?" I asked with insinuation.

"I haven't had any real plans for a long time," he said in a way that sounded like a confession.

"You didn't have any this morning?" I asked, raising an eyebrow. Okay... let's play this game.

"You saw that?" He seemed shocked.

"It's okay. So we kissed. It's not like you married me last night or anything. I was just... well, I don't know... I mean, it was my choice to kiss and fool around with someone I hardly knew. And of course, I should have realized you may be seeing other women. It's just... what we did, that really isn't me. I don't normally act that way. I want you to know that." Well, there it was... almost all in one breath.

"Woah. Okay. Slow down a minute," he said calmly. "I'm not seeing other women. Lindsay is just my neighbor. She asked me to fix her faucet... and I don't mean that in any metaphorical sense. I really enjoyed spending time with you last night and I'm hoping to get to know you a lot better. I'd love the opportunity to pick up where we left off, if I got the chance. But anyway... about you stalking me?" He said, half teasing.

"It wasn't stalking exactly. I came over earlier and cleaned up your place. I was hoping to see you, then later I saw the other woman sitting on your porch waiting for you and... sorry, I'm a mess. I feel like such an idiot right now." I really was coming unglued.

"Right. I can see how that might have looked. Well, how about you come over for a glass of wine and some dinner as a thanks for cleaning up for me? I really wasn't looking forward to waking up to all that and I so appreciate what you did. No one has ever done anything so nice for me before around here. We can do this whole dating thing in reverse if you want. Start with the kissing, then wine and dinner, and finally, hello. If you turn out to be a crazy stalker, I'm not too worried. I have 911 on speed dial."

He laughed. I was so glad he was having fun... at my expense, but one look into his beautiful soulful eyes and I just wanted to be with him even more.

Chapter Nine

Calvin

Lainey was so much fun to be with, and sexy as hell. I believed her when she told me she wasn't the type to sleep with anyone on their first date, but after spending the day with her, I knew she felt out of her element in Texas. More than anything I wanted her to love what I loved about the land. That huge sky, the fresh air, and the earnest people. She was a city girl and being so far from it could crush her if she didn't have a friend. I wanted to be that person for her because I had city in my veins too.

It felt strange to drive her the short distance to my ranch, but I didn't want to leave my truck at her place. We didn't speak for the one or so minutes it took to get home, and when we arrived, I invited her in. I tried to be as casual and relaxed as I could, but I felt the sexual tension between us mounting rapidly.

"So, do you have any preferences for dinner?" I asked.

"Not really. Do you have salad?" She seemed nervous.

"I do, but you might want to eat more than that. Ranch life can be tough, and you'll probably need to eat a lot more than you would in the city." She was slim, and beautiful, but even she could use a layer of softness. I loved women with a little to grab onto.

She laughed and said, "I don't eat a whole lot, but how about you make something easy. We've had a long day and I don't want you slaving away in the kitchen," she said politely. Somehow, I felt we weren't expressing the same level of honesty and risk we had the night before.

"Well, I love salmon with tarragon and thyme. How about an arugula with mandarin oranges, blueberries, and blue cheese with a balsamic vinaigrette? I can whip that up in about twenty minutes," I said with a smile. "And I'll open a bottle of cold Chardonnay while you watch me cook."

"Sounds great. I can help," she enthusiastically offered.

"Sure, can you make the salad?"

It was fun preparing the food together. When we were done, we set out some candles, and together with the fading sunlight, they illuminated our simple, yet romantic meal. We talked more, and I learned about her family and the tragedies she'd recently suffered. I told her a bit about me, but I still didn't want to divulge too much. If I was going to have a relationship with her, I wanted her to like where we were. I was afraid that if I confessed that I'd lived a life like hers too soon, she wouldn't understand how much living in the country meant to me.

After we'd finished and cleaned up, we went back on the porch and just looked at the night sky, making wishes on the few shooting stars we saw.

"What will you be studying when you go back to New York?" I asked, suddenly realizing I didn't even know what she was interested in. We'd spent most of our time talking about bucket lists and the differences between country and city living.

"I'll be studying for my masters in child psychology," she answered with a huge smile.

"Sounds like a great career. I'm guessing you like children?" I questioned.

"I love them, and so many kids need support these days. Life is just too fast for a lot of them, what with technology and accelerated learning. The next generation will have to solve the problems that we're all making for the world today, but that's a very daunting prospect for some. I feel drawn to help them if I can."

"That's a beautiful thing you're doing." And although it was, now I felt conflicted inside. I didn't want her to leave... ever. "You know I've only known you a day or so, but you're the best thing to come along since I moved here a few years ago."

"Thanks," she said coyly, "and you're the best thing about this place. I'm glad I came, even if it is just for the summer." She was being sincere. We'd known each other just over twenty-four hours and I was feeling so grateful we'd met.

"Well, that's very gracious of you to say, but I wouldn't say I was the best thing. You know, we have some amazing views here. If you'd like, we can take a horse ride around the perimeter tomorrow, and around your property too. You should at least know what you're getting yourselves into," I chuckled. I wanted to show her my world in all its majesty.

"That would be nice... if you have the time," she said. She seemed cautious in her reply, so I tried to reassure her with my warmest, widest smile.

"Oh, I have time. Lots of it. And if I didn't, I'd make time for you." And I definitely would for this pretty lady.

While all the talking was nice, as the night sky grew darker, I continued to feel the electricity grow between us, and I wanted her more and more. I couldn't stop thinking about feeling her body against mine and pleasuring her until she moaned with ecstasy. I hoped she didn't think the previous night was the one and only time we'd kiss and get as close as we did. My cock ached to be inside her, and I hoped it was the first of many nights we'd spend together. I felt a little nervous, but I had to try.

"It's getting late. Do you want me to walk you home, or would you rather stay and we could get a little more comfortable inside? I'd love to carry on our gazebo conversation if you can stay," I said, wiggling my eyebrows at her.

She laughed at my facial expressions then said, "Honestly, I want to stay here with you all night, but my head says I should have you walk me home," she confessed.

"Are you worried about the neighbors gossiping, or your dad? Is there anything I can say to make you change your mind? I make a mean breakfast... and coffee," I said, smiling and praying she'd give in.

"I'd love to stay, Calvin. I think you know I would, but I guess I'd need to talk with my dad first. You know, we just got here and all and for me to be sleeping over with the new neighbor on our second night here. It just seems... not right, you know what I mean? Him over there alone, and me staying here with you." She seemed uneasy about having to have a conversation with him about it.

"You don't have to tell him we're sleeping together. He'd probably want to be spared the details, anyway. We're just hanging out, having fun... falling asleep. He's a grown man. He can sleuth us out... or not."

"I guess," she said, hesitantly, biting her lower lip. God, so sexy.

"C'mon, Lainey. You're old enough to make your own decisions, and he practically booted us out the door earlier, anyway," I said in a low voice. "Honestly, I think he'll be okay with everything. Maybe it's you who are holding on too tight. Let go and enjoy your life, unless..." I leaned into her, moving closer until my body was pressed against hers. "Unless you aren't enjoying it?"

Her breath hitched at my touch. I knew she wanted me as much as I wanted her.

"No, I... I am enjoying life being with you." Her breathing became more rapid.

I pressed my face into her neck and whispered into her ear. "I want you in my bed... naked, so I can kiss and lick every inch of you." I wanted her to know how much I wanted to make her feel special... in so many ways.

"Oh, god," she whispered, closing her eyes as my lips trailed up and down her neck and along her jaw, her breath quickening with every movement. "How can a girl say no to an offer like that from a hot Texan like you," she said, smiling at me so sexily.

"I don't know the answer to that, and call me selfish if you want, but if I did, I'd never tell you," I chuckled.

"You are a wicked man, Calvin," she said with a laugh.

Fuck. I wanted her so bad. The hard bulge in my jeans was proof of that. I was so ready to show her what kind of lover a Texan man could be.

Chapter Ten

Lainey

Deep down, I knew Calvin was right, I was overthinking everything. I just needed to let go and let this—whatever it was becoming—grow. He finished his wine and while I was taking a sip of mine, he got up from his chair and stood next to me. Now at eye level, I couldn't help but notice the bulge in his pants. He was as ready for me as I was for him. There was a powerful magnetism that had attracted us and drew us together, and I couldn't resist giving into temptation. I stood up to be next to him.

"Calvin," I purred, trailing my hand along his chest, my eyes feeling heavy with lust. He looked at me with intrigue and knew immediately what I was leading up to.

"Shall we go upstairs?" he asked.

My pulse raced hearing those words. I was about to make love with this hunk of a man. He made me feel like nothing else in the world existed, but the two of us. My heart practically leaped out of my chest as he took my hand in his, as if to reassure me and let me know this was right for us. When we got to the bedroom, he led me in, closing the door softly behind us. He turned the lights down low, then looked at me from my head to my toes—undressing me with hooded, hungry eyes.

"God, you're so beautiful, Lainey. Your body, your spirit... everything about you is just... wonderful," he said seductively.

"It is?" is all I could think to say.

I watched him as he prowled slowly toward me across the polished wooden floor. It felt like he was stalking me like a tiger circled its prey and it felt a little strange, but it turned me on.

He planted soft, sensuous kisses along my neckline and across my collarbone, then smoothed my long blonde hair back from my head. We looked deep into each other's eyes and there was something unwritten, unspoken—I just felt an incredible connection with him. I leaned in and kissed his soft mouth, our tongues dancing together. He pressed against me and I felt his hardness grow as I rubbed my thighs against the bulge in his jeans.

He broke the kiss and smiled, his eyes sparkling in the soft light as I ground myself against his erection. He pulled my blouse over my head, then gently removed my bra, slipping the straps over my shoulders and expertly unclasping the back with one hand. He slipped it over my arms, exposing my breasts and his face lit up with delight.

"Magnificent," he praised, looking from one to the other before he leaned down and kissed each of my nipples, sending lightning bolts through my body.

"So are you," I teased, brightening the hot, seductive mood as I stroked his rock-hard cock, jutting out from his jeans.

His hands softly caressed my breasts, before delivering a quick, firm pinch to each nipple, making them hard and driving me wild. I threw my head back in pleasure after another pinch, then felt deliciously warm wetness as he sucked on one of my breasts. He licked and caressed the pebbling flesh until my core was dripping with need. The other hard nipple begged for his tongue, and he answered its call with tiny nibbles, sucks, and kisses. I tried to quieten my moaning, but he was driving me wild with desire. My wanton spirit took over, and I was so ready to let him take me on this incredible ride of pleasure.

I pressed myself harder against his stiffness, moving back and forth, wanting to feel his body closer to mine. He chuckled while kissing and sucking my breasts, returning my subtle thrusts.

"Mmmm, you feel good, too," he mumbled, his mouth full of my breast.

He stopped sucking, and we slowed our rhythmic grinding. He caressed my face as he worked his mouth up my chest and neck to my lips. He brushed a kiss across them, then along my jaw to nibble my earlobe. I felt the wetness soaking my panties.

He growled low in my ear, "I'm going to send you to the moon, darlin', you ready?" His breath was hot and seductive.

I was breathless. I had no words. All I could do was let out a moan and nod my agreement. His hand drifted downward, fingers stroking past my tummy to my pants. Slowly, he unbuttoned my jeans and gently coaxed me to the bed and guided me down to sit on it.

AMANDA HEARTLEY

"Lie down, Lainey," he whispered then slipped my jeans over my knees and tossed them to the floor. I was so wet from all his expert foreplay, I could feel it in the cool air on my inner thighs. He tucked his fingers into my panties and I raised my hips from the bed so he could tug them down, pulling them over my ass.

I prayed he wouldn't neglect the neediest part of me and I bucked my hips against his hand, hoping he'd touch me. He read my signals perfectly, stroking his thumbs over the wet fabric, pushing it against the soft petals of my sex then swiping them gently over my swollen bud. Pure pleasure flooded my brain as my body convulsed involuntarily, craving for more. He tugged again at my soaking panties and slid them down my legs, tossing them to the floor to join my jeans.

"Another pair for the collection," he joked, looking at me with smiling eyes and making me giggle at the weird, and somewhat perverted, thought of someone collecting my discarded underwear.

"What did you do with the pair I tossed in your lap last night, anyway?" I asked.

"Ah, they're safe with me," he said, nodding toward the drawer in his night stand.

I felt my eyes widen in disbelief. "They're not in there! Please say they're not!" I said incredulously.

"I went to bed alone last night, but I wanted to be close to you, the essence of you. So, yeah, they really are in there."

"Oh, God, no! Well, I hope you've got a Victoria's Secret in your poky little town," I said after I'd stopped laughing. "I'll be out of panties in no time at the rate you're scooping them up for your 'collection', and this is only day two!"

"Nope. We don't have those fancy places here. I think there's a store that sells some grammy panties that stop just short of the knee, but I don't wanna even think about those right now. I just want to taste you," he growled as he dropped to the floor beside the bed, pushing my legs apart and lowering his head between my thighs. "I want to feel your warm, sweetness against my mouth. I want to make you come."

"Oh... um... okay then," I said, giggling when I felt the scruff of his beard tickle my pussy, but the tickling soon turned to the most incredible sensation when I felt his soft lips against my lady parts. I grabbed his hair playfully and tried to pull him up to me, but he wasn't moving from where he was. The feeling of his mouth, licking and sucking my pussy lips sent rockets of pleasure coursing through my body. I twisted and thrust back at him with a tight, mounting tension that was sure to explode all over him.

"Oh, fuck, that's incredible. I'm... I'm going to..." I breathed frantically, unable to get the words out.

"Let it go, baby girl," he said as he kissed my stomach then went back down to my pussy and swiped his tongue up and down the folds. I felt a powerful orgasm building as he slid his tongue inside me and made quick stabs with the tip against my inner walls, then licked up to my swollen clit in a delicious rhythm.

That was it. I couldn't take any more, and a shiver sliced through my body. I didn't care if anyone heard me. I screamed out as my climax hit, coming hard all over his mouth and tongue. I heard him groan with delight as my juices spread across his face. Fuck, that was so hot hearing him enjoying my orgasm with me. I let my fingers dance in his hair as he kissed my thighs and stomach, letting me come down from my peak of ecstasy.

"Oh, god, that was amazing," I rasped, breathlessly.

"Why, thank you, ma'am," he teased in his sexy southern accent. I propped myself up on my elbows to watch him continue to love my lower body. I felt excitement mount again, but I wanted to return the favor before he had me rocketing to the moon once more.

I pulled at his hair. "Come on up here, cowboy. Your turn," I said as I tugged for him to come closer to me. I didn't have the energy to move him, but if he'd just come up off his knees and onto the bed, I'd show him how this city girl could make a country boy beg for mercy. He'd be crying for his momma by the time I'd finished with him.

He ducked out of his pants, leaving him completely naked with his stone hard cock waving about in the air and pulled out a square foil wrapper from one of the pockets. He tore it open with his teeth, throwing the foil to the floor and rolled the contents over his stiff length. He then pounced onto the bed and put one arm around me, pulling me closer.

"I want this to be all about you," he said as he put the other hand on my ass and lifted my leg around his waist. My pussy was wet, ready, and wanting—fully prepared for the invasion of his stiff cock. He pulled me to him and rocked his hips against my legs as he kissed me, deeply. I felt his erection, hard and slick, sliding in and out between my legs, grazing my pussy lips with each stroke.

I wanted him inside me more than anything as he positioned his thighs between mine, angling himself at my dripping wet center and I felt his cock nudging my lips apart. He groaned and looked into my eyes.

"I've wanted to make love with you since the minute we met," he said earnestly. "There's something about you that drives me crazy."

I'd never felt so adored as I wiggled my pussy on his stiff, wet cock. "Then take me," I breathed into his ear. "Take me now."

He pushed his hips closer to mine and slipped slowly inside me, both of us letting out a low moan. He moved gently and slowly at first and I felt his exquisite hardness filling me completely as we laid side-by-side. I kissed his hairy chest and the bulges of his pecs that were so perfectly defined as he rocked in and out of me. I planted wet kisses on his nipples, sliding my tongue over them and tasting his muskiness while he groaned in pleasure.

I wanted him inside me—harder, and deeper. I grabbed his ass and wiggled my way under him, my breasts grazing his chest and peaking with excitement again. I hoped he could feel what he was doing to me—my body electrified with intense pleasure as he shifted on top of me.

I wrapped my legs around him, my ankles resting on the backs of his thighs and feeling his exquisite fullness building me up to another unbelievable orgasm. He kept it slow and sensuous, planting sweet kisses on my neck and collarbone. His hot breath feathered across my chest and my aching nipples peaked in response as he took them into his mouth. I begged for more.

"I want you in me, deeper," I moaned.

"Like this?" he teased as he thrust himself hard into me.

"Oh my God, yes!" I yelped as the sudden invasion stung with a delicious kind of pain. I grabbed his back, shimmering with sweat and heat as he rocked hard into me again. "Ahhhh," I cried, holding him tight against me. My ankles pressed into his legs, spurring him on, then he propped himself up on his elbows and smiled a devilish smile.

"Hold on to me," he commanded as he started pumping in and out of me in long, hard strokes. I held onto his ass with both hands, pulling him into me as deep as I could. I spread my legs wide as he hammered his thickness in and out of me then felt a ball of sensation tighten in my stomach, and I knew I was about to come.

I gently bit his shoulder as he pulled out and bucked into me in a wonderful rhythm, gripping my hips as he moved at that sweet, torturous pace. It seemed every muscle of his body rippled as he brought himself in and out of me and my climax bloomed out of control. His eyes caught mine—full of heat, lust, and passion.

"Come for me, baby," he whispered. "I want to watch you come." That was it. I felt the mounting tension and my climax coming closer and closer until I couldn't hold it any longer. I exploded. Electricity running up and down my body, my brain awash with pleasure, crying out his name as my orgasm hit me like a freight train.

He slowed down, my fevered breathing becoming quieter as I came down from my climax. The air was thick with heat and the heady aroma of sex. I didn't know if it was love blossoming between us—it seemed far too soon for that—but Calvin was one of the most caring lovers I'd ever been with. As he let my passion still, I felt his thick length still lodged deep within me.

"Thanks for sending me to the moon, but it's no fun up here without you," I purred. He didn't protest when I rolled him onto his back and straddled him, pressing my slick folds onto his cock and sliding back and forth along its rigid length.

"Jeez, Lainey, that feels so good," he said, closing his eyes and letting out a low groan as I rocked my body against his. The head of his cock pushed against my lips, plowing them apart, making me gasp each time it rubbed against my clit, until I slipped it into my eager pussy once more. His dick towered deep inside me as I rode him, plunging down hard onto him then pulling myself up to the very tip of his rock-hard cock.

My butt cheeks slapped his thighs every time I came down on him, slowing my rhythm whenever I felt him twitch inside me. I wanted to make this last for him, but the more I rode him, the more I felt I was going to come again as he met my downward plunges by thrusting his hips up hard and holding my hips.

His eyes never left mine and looked so full of passion as he watched me make love to him. "Fuck, I'm coming, Lainey," he said, his breathing heavy. "I'm gonna explode." He closed his eyes and grabbed my hips with both hands, pulling me down hard onto him as he grunted out his orgasm. His body shook and convulsed as he thrust his hips hard against me, throwing his head back in the last throes of his climax.

"Not bad for a city girl, huh?" I asked, gently rubbing my hands up and down his chest and stomach. He smiled and opened his eyes, looking deeply into mine.

"Not bad. Room for improvement," he joked.

"What?" I said, slapping his arm. "You just had the best fuck of your life, mister country boy, and you know it," I said, returning his smile. I was just about jump off him in mock indignance at what he'd said when he raised his arms from my hips to my shoulders and pulled me down to him, crushing his soft lips against mine in a long, deep, passionate kiss. He threaded his fingers in my hair, cradling my head, and the other arm held me tight against him like he never wanted to let me go. I'd never felt so loved and desired in that moment.

When we eventually broke the kiss, I rolled off him and we laid on the bed next to each other, just basking in the afterglow of our love making. We didn't speak for a while—no words needed. I felt so comfortable lying naked next to him as his fingers traced the contours of my body while mine made lazy circles around his hard abs.

Eventually, he broke the silence. "I'm so happy you're here, Lainey. Words can't describe how good it is to be with you."

"You don't need words... let's just enjoy each other," I said, kissing his forehead. We laid there for a while longer, just talking, touching, kissing and being together then it started to get a little cold. I curled into his nakedness as I continued to swirl my fingers in the hairs on his chest and started to feel horny again.

"Do you want to shower with me?" I asked, my eyes wide and expectant.

"I'd love to," he answered.

"Also," I added, "next time... I mean, I hope there is a next time—" I felt anxious for a moment.

"Oh, there will be many, many next times," he assured me.

"Great. Well, just so as you know, I'm on the pill. I mean, I haven't been with a lot of men or anything, but you know... well, women should... it's better to be regular." *Holy shit. Shut up, Lainey!* Suddenly, I felt like a gynecologist.

"Oh... um... right," he smiled, stroking the hair from my face.

"Anyway, what I'm trying to say is I would love it if you came inside me next time. It's okay. I mean, I trust you." *Awkward.*

He kissed me.

"You can absolutely trust me, and I can't wait for that. Now, let's go take that shower," he said, playfully slapping my bare ass, sending delightful sensations to my still wet pussy.

We got up, naked and sweaty, and hit the shower. It felt great standing under the warm water. Just what my jellied muscles needed. The soap smelled amazingly fragrant as we lathered up our bodies. I turned around to wash him, noticing every rippling muscle of his body... and that vee... oh my God, I'd gone to heaven.

His skin was sunbaked a delicious shade of brown and he was lean from hard work. I was intoxicated by him—so flawless. As I moved my way down his body, I rubbed my soapy hands over his balls and cock, happy to see it growing hard again. I looked up at him and gave him a snarky smile.

"Well, well. What do we have here?" I asked as I lightly stroked him.

"Someone who's very happy," he smiled back.

He took the bar of soap from me, and gently turned me around, stopping me from stroking his growing erection. He soaped up his rough hands and ran them over my body, massaging my back and neck as he carefully washed every inch of me. I leaned back on him, feeling his stiff erection pressing against my ass. He lathered the soap into my neck then around to my chest, taking special care with each excited breast. His hand trailed downward as he soaped my stomach and hips. I wiggled my ass into him, urging him to go lower and felt his chest vibrate with his chuckling.

"You always so ready?" he laughed. "Let me enjoy the landscape first, before you go blowing my mind again."

I playfully rolled my eyes as he lathered up his hands again and placed the soap back into its holder. He surprised me by kissing my neck, then he licked it up to my earlobe and said in a low sexy voice, "You ready for this?".

He reached around my body and slid one soapy hand down over my tummy. I shivered in anticipation then it slid further to between my legs. His fingers slid up and down my folds, washing my pussy and exciting me again. He pressed his erection harder against my ass, making me buck into him and rubbing it up and down his hardness.

As soon as he'd covered my pussy in suds, he slipped his hand around my back and trailed his fingers down my spine. He cupped each of my cheeks then slid a fingertip down to my tight, puckered hole and rubbed it in small circles before slipping it gently inside.

My eyes widened to what felt like the size of dinner plates. "Oh my god," I breathed as he gently pushed his finger into my butt, filling me with intensely erotic sensations.

"Is this okay?" he smoldered.

"Mmm hhhmm," I blathered. "Just kinda surprising for a first date," I giggled as he slowly slid his finger in and out of my hole. No man had ever done that to me before, but it felt incredible. Calvin was turning out to be a very skilled lover.

"Well, it's not really a first date," he countered. "We did almost make out the first night I met you," he said with a small laugh.

His other hand reached around to my slick pussy and stroked my swollen lips before slipping inside. It felt like electricity flowed through my whole body, my legs trembling as I writhed on him, finger fucking my ass and pussy. I came so hard, mewling and purring as ecstasy gripped me, my legs almost buckling with my orgasm. He gently pulled his fingers out of me and two strong arms wrapped themselves around me, holding me up.

I felt his erection nudging my ass cheeks, and I spread my legs, bent forward and gripped the handrail fixed to the tile in front of me. The tip of his cock was slick with pre-come as he pushed past my ass cheeks and into my pussy. I let out a moan as he entered me deeply from behind and pumped in and out of me, filling me up again with his incredible body. It felt so good as I braced myself against the wall as his pace quickened.

I had to feel his body, next to mine, so I stood a little straighter and leaned into him as he pumped in and out of me. Two big hands were fondling my breasts and pinching my nipples as the water cascaded down on us. I lost my breath as I came again. I could barely think, my mind so full of desire. He thrusted hard and shouted my name as he came deep inside me, his hot come filling my pussy before trickling down my thigh.

I just wanted to stay with him inside me... forever.

AMANDA HEARTLEY

Chapter Eleven

Calvin

Lainey was fucking incredible. I wanted her to stay the night. Heck, I wanted her to stay forever, but I knew she had to do what was right for her. It wasn't late, probably only around nine o'clock, so not an indecent hour quite yet.

"I'd love for you to stay with me tonight, Lainey. I love being with you." I was being totally honest.

"Thanks," she smiled, but I could see that my proposal put her in an awkward position.

"Maybe you should call your dad and let him know we're going to watch movies or something?" I offered.

"Yeah, I want to call my dad, anyway, to make sure he's okay. I don't want him worrying you've got me chained up as a sex slave in your basement dungeon or anything," she said with a giggle.

"How did you know I had a dungeon?" I replied. "Anyways, I'd hate for him to be wandering over here just when we're... I mean, sure, call him and tell him I'll see him tomorrow to help out however I can."

She grabbed a sheet from the bed and we went downstairs to get her phone out of her purse.

"Hey, Dad," she said when he answered the phone, "Just checking you're ok over there. Calvin and I are having so much fun getting to know each other. Do you mind if I sleep over? We're going to watch some late-night movies and hang out... you know—kid stuff."

Well, not really kid's stuff, I thought to myself.

Her mood immediately changed, guess he agreed. We did pop in a movie, and after all our sexual exertions, I made us a snack and we snuggled up in front of the TV. When it was time to go to bed, she asked why I loved my ranch so much. It wasn't a hard answer to give her, but words really couldn't describe it.

"I'll show you in the morning, darlin'. I can't really articulate it well. I've had a very diverse life, which I'll tell you more about later, but compared to what I was doing before, this feels so much more right. In fact, for me, it's perfect. I'm working the land, using my body, feeding the people and the animals. It's a wonderful life." I hoped she understood.

"This feels right to me," she said as she spooned beside me. "I guess the rest of it will grow on me."

"But, it's just for the summer," I reminded her.

"Yeah, but my dad's here, and I can't leave him alone. It will be forever after I'm finished with school." This seemed to dampen her mood, so I changed direction.

"Nothing is forever, darlin'. It will all work out, just take it one day at a time," I counseled.

"You're right. No need to rush my life story." She smiled as she cuddled in deeper and yawned.

"Let's get some shut eye, we have a big day tomorrow." I kissed her again and soon she fell asleep.

She felt amazing, perfect and warm beside me. It made me realize just how much I'd been missing this in my life. I didn't just need any woman, I needed a woman like Lainey—strong, independent, kind, and fun. My heart swelled as I laid with her and fell asleep.

The next morning, we woke up, made love again, showered and had a light breakfast of eggs, toast, bacon and coffee.

"Where did you learn to cook?" she asked mid-bite.

"Believe it or not, I like to watch cooking shows and those YouTube cooking clips that pop up on Facebook." Lainey's face melted into mild shock.

"Really?" I didn't think she believed me.

"Really. It's fun to experiment, but I must confess, there isn't much to eggs and bacon. The toast part, though, that's where you really have a command of culinary skills."

She laughed. "It's just I don't cook much more than salad, cheese platters, and arranged fruit," she flashed a beautifully guilty smile.

"Cook?" I teased.

She shrugged her shoulders.

"You don't have to know how to cook in New York," she said, raising her nose in a gesture of faux snobbery.

"Is that so?" I asked as I gently tickled her side, which made her double over, giggling. "Well out here in the boonies, we grow our own food, shoot our own cows, and skin them right at the dinner table."

Her face lost all color, and the look on it was priceless. She was at a loss for words—such a city girl.

"It's El Paso, not Little House on the Prairie. We have delivery... sometimes, if Earl's truck is working."

She shook her head, still unable to say much then called her father to check in on him. His night seemed to have been a good one. We invited him to come on a horse ride around the perimeter of our properties, but he seemed very tired from the day before, telling her he was more interested in unpacking and getting settled.

He suggested we take a ride on our own and scope out the area. Later he'd have dinner for us and said he wanted to discuss his property with me and its possible uses. With her father happy, Lainey seemed to relax, like she was actually enjoying herself in Texas.

"You ready to head out and see what your dad has gotten you into?" I loved riling her up.

She rolled her eyes. "I guess."

"You'll like being out in the open air," I said as I cleared our plates. "It's rejuvenating."

"Seriously, I'm looking forward to it. I haven't been on a horse since I was a kid. I need to go home and freshen up though. Can we head out in an hour or so?" She batted her eyes unintentionally, but she was so adorable, especially since she didn't know she was so attractive.

"Well, you'll get unfresh again pretty soon, but sure, we'll head out in an hour. Make sure you wear sturdy shoes and jeans or something rugged. No skirts, little lady, or I won't be able to ravish you tonight," I winked.

"Oh, you think you will be ravishing me, do you?" She played along.

"A man can hope." I tipped my cowboy hat and gave her my biggest Texas smile.

She rolled her eyes at me, playfully and turned on her heels. "See you in an hour."

And with that, she walked out my front door. I hated to admit it, but she was starting to chisel away at my heart. I watched her walk to her house and felt a rush of excitement. Today was going to be an amazing day, and if all went to plan—and she wasn't too sore—I fully intended to ravish every inch of her gorgeous body again.

Chapter Twelve

Lainey

I walked home feeling like I was tripping on air. I was really starting to like Calvin more than I ever thought I would. He was a Southern gentleman, but also funny, kind, and smart. I couldn't stop thinking of him. It was so obvious he liked me as well. Men were bad at hiding their attraction, so I figured it was time for me to tell my Dad. While I'd only been in Texas three days, I wanted to explain what I was sure he already knew. When I walked in, he was busy setting things up in the kitchen.

"Hey, Dad," I said, casually.

"Hi, Lainey. How was your night, dear?" Such a dad.

"It was fun, and I really like Calvin. He's unlike any guy I've met before," I said with a giddy smile.

"Got a touch of the love bug then, do you?" Oh my God, the things he said sometimes.

"I think so." I was trying to be honest, but this was going to be a weird conversation to have with my father.

This was the kind of thing that women needed their mothers for. Those conversations where they discussed love and relationships. Usually, the talk included some reference of how their mother met their father, and how in love they were when they first started dating. Presumably, the discussion would then lead to caution about broken hearts and the natural fallibility of men, but would eventually end up with words of support and, eventually, congratulations. Conversations like those with a woman's father were simply awkward at best.

"Any words of advice?" I was goading him, I know, but I wanted a man's perspective if I could get it.

"Just keep your head up, honey, and remember how great you are. Other than that, you two have fun and see where it leads." And that was all the words he had for me though his advice was generally right on the money. He was an amazing father.

"Sounds like a plan. So, what are you going to do today while we're out trotting about the acres of our property?" I never thought I'd ever be trotting around anywhere on a horse, let alone on miles of our own land in the middle of nowhere.

"Thought I'd move us in and take an inventory of what we need to buy or replace." Always Mr. Matter of Fact.

"Can you torch my bedroom please?" I was being devilish.

"I won't set it on fire, but since our truck will be ready tomorrow, I'll go into town with you and find something more suitable. How's that sound?"

"Perfect! I don't think I can sleep in there until all that pink princess stuff is gone." I was playing with him.

"Good thing you haven't been sleeping in there, then," he winked. Oh, god. More awkward moments with my dad.

"Right, well, I need to freshen up and get ready for our ride. You keep on keepin' on, Dad." *Why did I just say that?*

I felt so unbalanced by everything, but Dad gave me a cheery thumbs up and with that, I was off to find something sexy yet practical to wear for my outing with Calvin.

Chapter Thirteen

Calvin

When Lainey returned she was wearing a pair of jeans that made her ass look amazing. Her shirt was cut to expose the top of her incredible tits and frankly I just wanted to rip the clothes off her and throw her down on the couch—but I was a gentleman. There'd be plenty of time to ride each other later, but right now, the horses awaited us.

"Oh, my God!" she exclaimed, "I don't remember horses being so big." She seemed nervous.

"Don't worry. That's Lucky. She's the tamest horse in the stable. I'll teach you a few of the basics and she'll follow your lead."

I could tell Lainey was nervous when I took her out to the stables to get the horses, but she was hiding it well.

"You sure she won't buck me off or anything?" she laughed, trying to cover her fear.

"Nope, she never has and never will," I said as I approached Lainey. "Here, let me help you up."

I helped lift Lainey onto the saddle and as soon as she was on top of the horse her fears seemed to dissipate. We took off with a picnic lunch packed in the saddle bags and I showed her how to control the horse along the way as we rode off into the alfalfa fields. While some people might find them boring, being nothing but row upon row of green weeds, I explained my choice of crop while we trotted through the fields.

"I got into alfalfa because I saw an untapped niche to support other ranchers in the area. I didn't want to run a dairy or a meat farm and my soil wasn't good enough for mass production of other crops, so I thought alfalfa would be a good business as it's an incredibly nutritious livestock feed. I sell at a fair price and have a high yield, so we're doing well. The only hard part is the fact that we turn over the land every six to eight weeks. I end up hiring a lot of people to work with me and I also have some permanent staff who are on vacation this week." I thought I might be boring her with the details, but she looked interested, even if she was only being polite.

"And what about the garden at the back of your house? What are those vegetables for?" I was excited that farming had piqued her interest.

"I grow my own food. That way I know what's in it and it's always fresh. I only have to go to the store to buy stuff I can't grow or make myself." I laughed at myself for sounding a bit intense.

"That's cool. I don't know how much growing we'll be able to do. I had a cactus once. It lived like six weeks or something," she said with a sheepish grin.

"You're definitely going to need some help then, or you might starve." I tried not to be too harsh.

"Oh, I don't know about that. There's that marginally good grocery store in town, and I can always steal from your yard," she retorted with a devious smile on her cherry red lips.

We rode out for several hours, just taking in the beautiful view in the fresh air of the countryside. She seemed overwhelmed, but also exhilarated by the horseback ride. However, I could tell she was getting uncomfortable with all the riding, so I suggested we stop and have our lunch.

We rode over to my favorite part of the property where there was another gazebo. In the wide-open expanse of the ranch, it felt like there was no one else in the world around us. I remembered growing up as a child there where my friends and I would ride the horses, or a tractor out to the spot and play games among the trees. There was an abandoned trailer on the west of the property that had been long forgotten, and I'd considered taking a ride out there for our picnic until I thought about the likely condition of the old tin.

I recalled my father saying the trailer belonged to one of my uncles who'd lived there once upon a time, but I only remembered it being rusted and full of holes and spiders. It was a perfect fort for young boys to grow up playing in though, and over the years it had been a gangster hideout, an old west homestead, and a military fortress. You name it, that rusted, broken down heap had been it. It felt like the entire world could be encapsulated in that small space and I wanted her to understand the magic I'd grown up with.

"We can have our lunch here," I said, stopping my horse.

"Oh, thank God. I think my butt is going to fall off." She gave me a beleaguered smile.

"I'm pretty impressed for someone who hasn't ridden a horse in years. You've managed to stay on for over two hours," I congratulated her.

"That's probably because I can't feel my legs." She looked hot and weary.

"Well, I've made us a delicious lunch, so you'll be feeling better soon," I said as I hopped off my horse and strolled over to hers.

I offered her my hand and helped her down. She was really sore, and I worried whether I'd be able to persuade her to get back on it again. Maybe a little massage would help.

I removed the blanket and picnic from my saddlebag and spread the blanket across the floor of the gazebo. Lainey toed out of her riding boots then I took her hand and helped her into the space.

"This looks amazing, thank you," she said as she sat down and crossed her legs, Indian style. She seemed genuinely grateful.

"I really wanted to bring you out here. This place is very special to me," I confessed.

"How so?" she asked as she popped a grape between her lips.

"I grew up out here, this was my home away from home. Me and my friends had a blast making up stories and playing in that old tin heap." I smiled at her and pointed toward the trailer off in the distance.

"It would be a cool place to play I guess," she said, trying to see where I was coming from.

"Most of my friends are gone now," I said with a note of sadness.

"They didn't die or anything, did they?" Her face softened.

"One did. He was killed in Afghanistan. One moved away when their farm went bankrupt, another is in jail for stealing a car. It was a dumb teenage prank, but he got the maximum sentence. We all just drifted apart. It feels good to come here sometimes, just to relieve the memories." I was quiet and reflective when she took my hand in hers.

"Well, now, we're making new memories," she replied, flashing her beautiful smile. She shifted her body, obviously still in pain from the ride.

A massage this evening was definitely in order... and I was just the man for that job.

Chapter Fourteen

Lainey

Our picnic was beautiful. The run-down trailer in the middle of nowhere was quite shocking, but hearing Calvin talk about his childhood was endearing. I understood why he'd brought me out to his special place, where the wind kissed the grassy Texas plains. It was all very beautiful, and I enjoyed the time we spent together there. After our delicious meal, we mounted our horses again. I didn't think there was any way I could get into the saddle, but as soon as I settled in, it wasn't so bad.

"It's time we see your property now and get an idea of what you and your dad have bought," he smiled.

"I shudder to think," I quipped.

We traveled farther down the hill, and he told me about how his previous neighbors had been there for many years before us. He took us to a little lake on our ranch I didn't even know we had. I couldn't believe it—we had our own little lake. It wasn't big enough to put a boat on, but it was a nice little watering hole, nevertheless.

Ducks swam on the surface, apparently taking a rest from their annual migration, according to Calvin. We got off our horses, and he showed me the tadpoles and frogs just under the surface of the water. We acted like kids again, laughing and giggling, then he took off his shirt and stripped out of his pants, leaving himself standing in just his underwear. I didn't know why I was shocked to see him practically naked. Lord knows, I'd seen plenty of it the night before, but not out in the open air like this.

"Whatcha doin' there, nature boy?" I asked.

"Fancy a dip? The water is perfect this time of year," he said as he ran and dived into the water.

"Can't you get rickets from standing pools of rancid water?" I asked sarcastically.

"No, that's not how you get rickets, but you can get Legionnaire's disease." he said as he splashed water up on me.

I backed away just in time.

"Hey!" I shouted. "You almost got me wet."

"That's the point. I want to make you wet," he said with a wink. Damn he was sexy, then he splashed again.

"What kind of disease was that?" I asked.

He started walking out of the lake and headed toward me, looking a little ominous.

"You only get it if you swallow the water, however, your clothes will get very wet if you don't take them off now," he said in a playfully menacing tone.

"Why?" I backed away cautiously.

"Because when I reach you, I'm going to throw you in the drink," he exclaimed as he rushed for me.

Instinctively, I ran. He was too fast for me though and caught me easily. Sweeping me up into his arms like a baby, he carried me to the lake.

"NOOOO!!!" I yelled.

"You'd better get that shirt off then, before I toss you in," he threatened again.

"Wait, wait, put me down and I will," I said, acting as if I was a damsel in distress.

I resigned myself to the fact that it could be a fun game and took off my shirt and jeans just in time before he picked me up and tossed me out into the freezing cold water. I wanted to be irritated by that, but it wasn't as freezing as I thought it would be, and it was fun swimming and splashing about with him.

There I was, almost naked in the middle of the vastness of our ranch, with a beautiful blue sky, and a man I had to admit to myself I was falling in love with. He caught me again as I was treading water after swimming out to the middle. He pulled me into his arms from behind me as the water lapped around us and I felt his hardness through his underwear jutting into my back. I turned to him and wrapped my legs around him, making sure my pussy sat right on top of his hardening erection.

"Having fun?" I asked as I wiggled on his engorged cock.

He leaned in and kissed me. I returned the kiss as the water gently lapped around us. The cool, fresh air tickled our skin as we kissed and wriggled on each other. I wanted to make love to him on the banks of the lake like they did in the movies, but frankly, my body was too sore from riding horses all day, and him all the previous night, so we just fooled around and enjoyed being close to each other.

After we'd kissed and groped to the point where we'd either have to stop or make love, I suggested a swimming race across the pond instead. Of course, he beat me, but I didn't do too badly. I only came in a few seconds behind him.

"Ha! You're a good swimmer." he proclaimed.

"I won third place in our school swim championships, so I should be." I gloated.

"Well, then. That's it, we'll have to swim out in this lake more often. Maybe you can beat me one day," he goaded.

"I'm just off my game because of the horseback riding and sex. I'm not used to either, but I'll win next time," I said with more bravado than belief.

He got out of the lake and started to dry himself with his shirt.

"Why are you getting out?" I asked.

"It's getting late and we've hardly seen any of your property yet. There's more, so we should get going before it starts getting dark." Now he was being Mr. Sensible, just like my dad—which wasn't entirely all bad.

"Okay," I sulked.

"There'll be plenty of time to swim another day." He still sounded like my father.

We watered the horses from a spout not far from the lake. They'd been resting in the shade, but needed water and carrots, then it was back on them... ugh. The second go around hurt much worse than the first and my legs were screaming in pain, but it was a good kind of pain. I felt my city muscles hardening and my body being pushed. I figured this was what bodies were made for—being outside and being active. When I thought about it, I regretted how soft the hustle and bustle of the city had made me.

As we circled around our ranch, we saw nothing but open land. Not much of it was being used for anything and there were crumbling buildings dotted all over the place. First, we came upon a dilapidated hay barn, lopsided and falling down. Next, we passed a barn with a massive hole in the roof, and a stable which had one whole wall missing.

"What happened to all these old buildings?" I asked Calvin. Everything seemed so desperate and neglected.

"The prior owners didn't need them anymore. They were elderly and just couldn't keep up with the maintenance," he said as we trotted past.

"Seems kind of sad," I shared with him.

"Yeah, but it's a lot of work running a ranch, and those old folks couldn't do it anymore," he added.

There was no way my father would be able to keep up with maintaining all these building either, and as much as I wanted to repair it all, I wouldn't be able to do it on my own. Soon I'd be concentrating on school and getting my master's degree. There wouldn't be time to worry about worm-rotted wood. Although they looked so forlorn, the idea of tearing them down seemed a crime.

I remembered a story I'd read about a woman in California who was an animal rights activist of some sort. She rescued farm animals and raised awareness by teaching disadvantaged city kids about their lives by letting them visit her farm to learn about them. She had a place on the west coast, another in Tennessee, and they were very popular for education and inspiration.

I wondered if I could combine my desire to work with troubled children as a psychologist and use the ranch as well. Maybe I could create something similar by making it a summer camp for troubled kids. My life was peachy compared to theirs, but even I felt the positive effects of clean air and the open country after just one day. I imagined they'd feel the same, interacting with animals, growing their own food, and camping under the stars.

Suddenly, I felt energized and excited about the prospect of giving back to the community while still working in New York and Texas. I looked at Calvin riding ahead of me, I was so excited about my new idea that I wanted to share with him. I had a lot to plan and work out if this crazy notion was going to take root.

"Is it hard to get permits to use the land as a non-profit?" I asked casually.

"I'm not sure, I've never tried. What's brewing in that pretty head of yours?" He must have seen the scheming look in my eyes.

"Not too much just yet, I was just thinking of ways to use the land to help others. We could renovate those buildings and use them as part of a learning project for troubled children."

He looked at me, stunned and speechless for a moment. I let the silence play out for a minute as we rode.

"That's very ambitious," he said after a minute.

"It is, but I think it's something I can do, and I'd be able to work here and in New York." I said with a flirty smile.

"I think that's a wonderful idea," was all he added.

"We'd have to apply for grants and hire a bunch of people to help out," but I was mostly talking to myself.

I mulled over everything I might need to do as we continued along the perimeter of the property. It was an endless sea of dead grass, broken fencing, and miles of disuse. It would be a lot of work, but I felt it would be so worth it in the end.

When we got back to our house, Dad had just set the dinner table and the welcoming aroma of seared steak, biscuits and gravy hit us the minute we walked in the door.

"Wow, that smells amazing," Calvin commented.

"That does smells good, Dad. When's dinner?" I was starving.

"Right now. Just wash up and I'll serve," he said jovially.

Over dinner we told Dad what we'd seen, and Calvin shared some ideas he had about using some of the land as an organic farm. Dad would have to hire people no matter what he decided, but growing produce might be an option. He'd been considering keeping bees and, of all things, candle making. That surprised me, but maybe now he was retired, it was his chance to bring out his creative side.

I shared my idea about creating a summer sanctuary with barn animals and crops for inner city kids, and Dad loved the idea. I thought Calvin still believed my idea was half-baked, but I didn't care, I was ready to start on my plan.

"Don't you think that's going to be a lot of work, honey?" Dad asked cautiously.

"Everything out here is a lot of work, Dad. I'm beginning to learn that's the nature of country living." I was being as earnest as I could.

Calvin chuckled and said, "Today wasn't even working, Lainey," he teased.

"And I feel like a locomotive ran over my ass, so sitting on this aching butt and filling out a few forms for a grant proposal should be a lot easier than riding around the prairie on horseback with you," I said, smiling, and rubbing my sore backside. They both laughed, but I wished it was Calvin doing the rubbing.

But that would have to wait for another time.

Chapter Fifteen

Calvin

It was clear from her wincing and rubbing of her aching joints that Lainey needed rest, so I returned to my ranch after a wonderful dinner with my new neighbors. I'd had a great day with her and I had no desire to start working, even though I knew my head had been in the clouds for the last few days and there was a lot of business I had to get down to. I called Lainey later that evening and asked her to go out on the town with me on the Wednesday night and since it was only Monday, it gave us both a little time to catch up on things.

I wasn't surprised, but I couldn't deny I was disappointed when she told me she had to go back to New York. She'd received her acceptance to NYU and sounded so excited about starting her Master's degree. She hoped to pitch her idea of a rehabilitation ranch to her professors with an independent study, spending half her time in Texas and the other half in New York, and the reality of her life away from Texas... and me, started to sink in—she really was going to leave at some point. I hated the idea of her being so far away, even it was only for a few months. I felt devastated at the thought of not having her around.

While I'd have loved to have kept her here for myself, the thought of her being able to travel back and forth was an interesting one, and at least I wouldn't lose her completely. I agreed to see her later and hung up the phone. She assured me she'd call me when she had all the details and would see me before she left.

The rest of the day was a total wipeout as I couldn't stop thinking about her and when she called back later that night, it felt like she'd been gone for years. I was a grown man, and I knew I was being absolutely ridiculous. I couldn't even go half a day without her? She said she was leaving for New York the next morning and apologized about the short notice, but she had to pack for the trip and couldn't see me that night.

I was disappointed, of course, but I offered to drive her to the airport and she accepted enthusiastically. At least I'd get to see her one more time before she left, but the fact she couldn't make time to see me knocked me off kilter a little. I knew it was crazy—maybe even possessive—to worry about that, but I had to accept we'd only known each other a few short days, that she had ambitions in her life and perhaps they, and New York, would always be a conflict for us.

I guess I'd known that from the start, but the stark reality was hitting me hard and I missed her in my bed that night.

AMANDA HEARTLEY

***

On the ride to the airport the next morning, we talked about the future, maybe more me than her. I knew how crazy it was to be thinking about a future with a woman I'd known less than a week, but that was exactly what I was doing—I glanced in the rear-view mirror before changing lanes and I didn't like what I saw. Normally, I was a strong, confident guy, but what stared back at me was the face of someone who'd officially gone insane.

"How long are you planning to be in New York?" I asked.

"Oh, I'll be home on Sunday," she cheerfully replied. "I have a couple of meetings at the school and I'm planning to see some old friends while I'm in town. Can you keep an eye on Dad for me? He hired an overseer to work on the property, so he'll be there, but it's nice to have another pair of eyes checking in on him," she smiled.

"Be my pleasure. I hope to hang out with him and we can sink a couple of beers together. He's led an interesting life and I really like the guy." She laughed, and I felt a warm-hearted connection with her.

"Great, but don't you two go getting yourselves into too much trouble," she playfully warned me. "I've seen the movies about cowboys whooping it up down at the saloon, drinking whiskey, playing poker and taking girls upstairs to be, shall we say... *entertained*," she said, her fingers making air quotes.

I laughed out loud at the thought of me and her dad hitting the town and barging our way through the swing doors of some saloon doors with our six-shooters and a gun belt.

"In case you didn't notice, our little town isn't exactly the wild west, Lainey," I chuckled. "It's much more like Harlequin Western Romance. Anyway, what did your father decide to do with the ranch? I'm surprised he's hired someone already, that was so quick."

"Oh, right. Well, turns out he'd already spoken with someone local before he bought the place. They discussed some ideas for the land yesterday and Dad was so impressed, he hired the guy there and then."

"Really? Maybe I know him if he's from around here?" I said, inquisitively.

"His name was Jake. That's all I can tell you. He was already at the kitchen table when I came down from my room after I'd packed my suitcase. Does that ring a bell?" she asked.

"Not sure. I know a Jake who's the foreman at old Johnson's place. Could be him," I replied. "I'll find out, though. I'd hate for your dad to be taken for a ride."

"Would you?" she said, grabbing my arm and squeezing it. "I'd hate that, too, especially with me being gone. Anyway... I mentioned my proposal again to both of them, and the details of the plan I've been working on. You know, the specifics about a working barn for rescued animals, a place to hold a summer camp for underprivileged city kids for a start, and I'm so excited they agreed to it," she said, a wide smile beaming across her pretty face.

"That's great, Lainey. I'm so happy for you and I'm totally impressed you've got this idea of yours off the ground so quickly. You sure do get things done once you put your mind to something, don't you?" I was truly blown away by her drive and ambition to help people less fortunate than herself—as if I didn't love everything about her already.

"Why, thank you, Calvin," she said, beaming with obvious pride and staring at me wide-eyed as I drove us down the highway.

I took my eyes off the road momentarily and smiled at her. "You're more than welcome. Have you and your dad decided what to do with the rest of your land, yet?"

She wrapped both her arms around my right arm, snuggled her head against my shoulder then said, "Well, I don't know anything about anything out here, but they discussed it and thought the most sustainable business would be crops like wheat or sorghum... whatever that is, and Dad mentioned bees again, of course. He really wants to keep bees, for some reason."

"Nothing wrong with keeping bees," I said.

"Ya think so?" she said, raising her head and looking at me intently. "Those fuckers sting... and I know... first-hand," she said, somewhat indignantly.

"Do tell," I turned to smile at her, then she snuggled back into my shoulder, facing the road ahead.

"Well, a couple of years ago, I was out shopping... just minding my own business, you know," she started. "Just walking down Fifth Avenue like a girl would, looking in the store windows at all the pretty things on display... when suddenly a bee snuck up behind me, tried to fly through the glass I was looking through, bounced off and fell straight down my cleavage... and I mean... like, right between my tits, if you know what I mean?"

"Um, yeah... I can picture those... I mean, that scenario," I said with a grin. She giggled at my innuendo and continued her story.

"Right. So now I'm freaking out. I didn't know what to do. I had a bug in my bra that could sting one of my tender lady parts at any moment. I didn't know exactly where it was, other than some tickling as it buzzed around my boobs trying to get out, and I didn't want to pat my clothing or put my hand down there and annoy it any more than it was," she continued.

My body started shaking uncontrollably as I began to laugh at the scene she was painting in my head. She sat up straight and slapped my arm. "Calvin! It wasn't funny," she said, indignantly.

"I'm sorry," I said. "But you obviously survived to tell the tale. So, what did you do?"

"Well, duh! Of course I survived, but I was going batshit crazy in the middle of Manhattan at the time. I don't do bugs, so have a little sympathy, will ya?" she pleaded, nestling into my arm once more.

"I'm really sorry for laughing, Lainey, but you have to admit, it does sound funny to someone else. Oh, and just a quick heads-up... you'd better get used to bugs out here. We've got lots of them... big ones too. Anyway, tell me what happened. I want to hear the end of this story," I said with a chuckle.

"Bugs? Eeeww!" she squealed, and I laughed again. She was such a city girl. "Well, I moved slowly so as not to annoy the bee then looked around to see if I could find a woman close-by who could help me, but at that moment, there were none. All I saw in the immediate vicinity was a middle-aged guy with glasses and bushy eyebrows smiling at me. He looked like a total pervert and so not on my list of potential help, then I turned around and saw a news stand run by an old guy with a beard and just hoped for the best," she recalled.

"Okay, so a middle-aged guy with eyebrows is a pervert, and an old guy with a beard is okay?" I interrupted. I glanced sideways for a second and saw her looking at me intently, her eyes narrowing like she was about to kill me.

"You're not getting it, are ya, country boy?" she said with a small smile. "I had a live bee down my bra, dude! Imagine for a minute you had a bee down your shorts. In a situation like that, there is no time for too much thinking. What was I supposed to do? Run background checks on everyone around me before I asked them to help? Hmm?"

She paused, as if waiting for my answer, but all I could do was open my mouth and try to form a sentence. It seemed like I'd pressed her buttons and she was turning out to be quite the feisty lady. A side of her I hadn't seen before, but I had to admit, I really liked it.

"I... uh... I..." I was lost for words and just shrugged my shoulders, not wanting to rile her up anymore.

"No," she continued without waiting for my reply. She seemed to be on a roll and I didn't want to get in her way. "I used my woman's intuition and chose the closest person who I thought was the least likely to molest me. Now, get with the program and my predicament," she said, half-exasperated, but still smiling... thank God.

"Okay, okay. Sorry I asked," I said in a conciliatory tone, taking my hands off the wheel for a second and holding them up in surrender.

She pulled herself back into me and gave my arm a tight squeeze. "I'm only playing with you, Calvin. I'm not the kind of girl to be hollering at her man. Now, do you want to hear how the story panned out, or are you going to keep flapping your lips all day?" she said, then burst out laughing at her irony. God, I loved to hear her laugh... and I loved being around her.

"Um, sure. I'll keep quiet, ma'am," I said, tipping my hat.

"Oh, don't you ever keep quiet," she whispered. "I love hearing you speak with that sexy southern drawl of yours... especially in the bedroom," she winked, squeezing my thigh.

"No, ma'am," I tipped my hat again in mock deference. "Now, about the ending to the story?"

"Oh, right. Yeah, well I sidled nervously over to the news stand, petrified I'd get stung at any minute. Luckily, there were no other customers there and all I could do was point furiously at my cleavage, totally wide-eyed, and whisper, *'Bee!'* The guy raised his head and looked at me like I was insane, so I had to repeat myself with a little more detail. I said a little louder, *'There's a bee in my bra, can you help me get it out?'"*

Well, the guys eyes lit up like a Christmas tree, then he looked nervously up and down the street before he guided me away from public stare and under cover inside his stand. There, he put on his glasses that had the thickest lenses I'd ever seen in my life and said, *'May I look?'* I just nodded, wanting that sucker out of there, then he slowly pulled the neck of my blouse toward him and peered inside, looking left and right. Then he let it go and pulled my sweater the same way. I remember rolling my eyes, staring at his ceiling and thinking I'd die of embarrassment. Lord knows what anyone would've thought if they'd poked their head around the corner at that moment. It was like Professor Frink meets high school cheerleader. Very weird and definitely not erotic."

"The dirty, lucky bastard," I chuckled.

"No, he was the perfect gentleman, actually. He didn't look overly long or feel me up at all. He asked me to stay perfectly still then carefully slid his hand inside my sweater and pulled it out with the bee crawling on his finger. It spread its wings, flew out the door and the drama was over. So anyway, to cut a long story short, because of that frightening incident, me and bees—well, bugs in general—we don't get along."

"That was cutting a long story short?" I looked at her quizzically for a moment. "If that was a guy telling it, it would probably go something like, *'A bee flew down my shirt. Someone got it out. The End.'*" She slapped my arm again, and we both laughed. "So, getting back to you and your dad's plans for crops and those pesky bees, does he know about any of that stuff?"

"He knows some. He's done a lot of research about running ranches and farms, and he knows how most people rely on imported food, but he thinks there's a market for local farms to provide healthy, organic food as well. Some folks will only buy organic, anyway, and you never know what could happen. Foreign crop failures, global warming or, forbid the thought, wars could mean these local ranches supplying their communities. Dad's decided he wants to make fresh honey and either sell or rent bees to farmers for natural pollination of their crops. He's set on the idea and I think it would be a great learning opportunity for the kids as well, so they can understand sustainability and the importance of bees to the eco system," she explained.

It seemed well thought out to fill a niche, and the plan sounded a good one. There weren't a lot of beekeepers in the area and it would be a sustainable business if he didn't commercialize. I was very impressed with what they'd come up with.

"That's a really good idea, and I'd be glad to help in any way I can. Now, are you going to be okay in New York all on your own?" I asked sincerely.

She looked up at me and laughed.

"Well, I only left New York about two weeks ago, so I'm pretty sure my friends will still remember me and, hopefully, still like me. I don't think I've lost any of my street savvy... yet," she said with a snide little smile.

"You never know. New York's a big city, and then there's King Kong and Godzilla to worry about," I teased, trying to hide the fact I was really going to miss her.

"I'm not staying at the Biltmore Hotel. King Kong wouldn't think of going there again anyway since it turned out so badly for his last time and um... it was gutted. It's a Bank of America now," she joked.

"Where are you staying?" Somehow, I needed to know where she was going to be.

"I'm staying at the Wythe Hotel near Brooklyn. It's a cool place."

"I've heard of it," I let slip.

"You have?" She seemed too shocked to say any more.

"I... have." I decided not to go deeper, so I changed the subject. "I'm gonna miss you." I was being stupid crazy, but I needed her to know she meant something to me—something more than just a casual fling.

"It's only been less than a week," she said. "You're not going to miss me when you get back to your ranch."

Truthfully, I was kind of expecting her to dismiss my heartfelt comment and brush off what the last few days had been for us. Maybe she felt something, too, and it was just her way of coping with our impending separation.

"It feels like longer," I confessed. "In a good way."

"It does," she said, looking down as if she was deep in thought then suddenly, she sat bolt upright in her seat and leaned back against the passenger door. "Well, why don't you join me in New York and I can show you around my town," she said, excitedly. "God knows, I need to visit Victoria's Secret and buy their entire stock of panties before I come back to Texas," she said with a huge grin on her face.

While on the face of it, it seemed a reckless idea, it was also an exciting one. I felt her watching me intently while I drove as if she could see me seriously considering the idea. I found it a little unnerving that she could read my mind and push my buttons after such a short time of knowing me, but she never let up the pressure and started to hard sell the crazy concept to the emotional side of my brain.

"You could buy a ticket. I don't think the flight is sold out, and we could buy you some proper city clothes when we get there. We can't have you walking around the place like Crocodile Dundee just rode into town," she enthused.

"Crocodile Dundee? He's Australian," I replied. I needed more time to think this over, so I kept the conversation going.

"Right, but he wears a hat and boots just like yours. Us city folk aren't used to seeing cowboys in town—apart from the one in the Village People—but everyone knows Crocodile Dundee," she joked.

"Well, I don't know—" I started.

"Oh, come on, Calvin, it'll be fun," she interrupted. "You took me on a wild adventure and now it's time for me to take you on one. Say yes. Live a little, be wild and spontaneous, you're only young once... and any other cliché that comes to mind. It'll be expensive, but you have a whole alfalfa field... and I can help with money if you need any. Come on," she said, her eyes sparkling with excitement. Then she leaned forward and grabbed my arm with both hands, tugging it back and forth like a petulant child having a tantrum, but all with that naughty, sexy smile on her face.

I had to admit, it was a thrilling prospect and a totally off-the-wall crazy idea, yet, infinitely do-able. I could have my foreman handle the ranch alone for a few days, and I had more money than I could use in a lifetime, so there really was nothing to stop me.

Lainey still didn't know I was a multi-millionaire, and she had no idea I was a big business tycoon in a prior life. The tingle of excitement this outrageous trip gave me was way more inspiring than the idea of going back to the ranch to work as usual and wait out the time Lainey was gone from my life.

What piqued my interest most was the idea of sharing Lainey's New York with her. I'd shown her my ranch and the land I loved, but it would be amazing to see New York through her eyes. I'd lived there on and off with my ex-wife, but her version of the city was empty and self-absorbed with her love of the most expensive restaurants and the most influential people. Despite all that was wrong with the idea, the more I considered it, the more my heart said I should do it—and that's what I said.

"Yes, okay." I looked at her intently, unsure of the consequences my decision might bring.

"Are you serious?" she asked, disbelieving what she'd just heard, her eyes as big as saucers.

"I think so. It's totally insane and completely irresponsible, but I can't think of a solid reason not to go," I confessed.

"Oh my god, this is amazing," she squealed, an eardrum-shattering squeak that left my ears ringing for a moment. She put her hands to her face and bounced up and down in her seat like a kid. It made my heart melt to see her so happy.

"I don't know, but if you do that again, I may be too deaf to join you," I said, playfully rubbing my ears.

"Oh, sorry. It's just that I'm so excited you're actually coming with me, I could pee myself, but I'll be okay in a minute," she whispered, the big smile never leaving her face.

"Do you think your dad will be okay? I'll have my foreman check in on him every day," I suggested.

"Dad's gonna be fine, and I forgot to tell you, I think your friend, Lindsay, has stopped over a couple of times while we've been out riding. Dad mentioned it casually this morning, and I know the two of them are going to have lunch together tomorrow."

"Oh, really?" I said, raising my eyebrows in genuine surprise. I never saw that one coming, but secretly, I was glad that the two of them were hitting it off. I didn't want to be called over for any more plumbing jobs. "Well, I hope she'll be gentle with him," I chuckled. *God, does the poor man know what he's letting himself in for? She'll literally eat him alive.*

"What do you mean?" she quizzed.

"Oh, nothin'. She's a good friend... and a good woman too. Just hope he can handle her," I replied with a smile.

"You don't mean... yes, you do, don't you?" she said.

"I'm not saying anything. I think it's great your father is making friends," I said with a wry smile.

"Lindsay? And my dad? You're not serious? Oh my god! I hadn't thought about them in that way. Thanks for grossing me out, Calvin!" she said, holding her head in her hands. "Things a daughter shouldn't know... or even think about... ever!"

"Maybe they're just going to have lunch and get to know each other," I suggested to try to calm things down, but I figured it was too late. I'd said too much already.

"Like we got to know each other better?" she said, her hands still covering her face.

Oh, shit. That's when I realized I should have stopped talking minutes before. It was time to back-pedal... fast. "No, I'm sure it's nothing like that.

C'mon, stop thinking about it and think about where you're going to take me in New York instead or you'll give yourself nightmares. I'm sure he'll be missing you already."

She sat upright in her seat again and looked at the road ahead. "Well, he does seem pretty excited about everything he has planned. His beekeeping stuff, making new... *friends,*" she said, turning to me with those darn air quotes again, just to remind me what an idiot I'd just been. "I don't think he'll miss me at all. In fact, this morning he was like *'Bye, honey, have fun. I'll Skype you in a few days.'* which kind of had a *'Bye, honey. Now, get out of here so I can live my new life.'* sort of vibe to it," she laughed. Phew, I was out of the woods now she had that beautiful smile going on again.

"Great, well we should call him and let him know what we're planning to do." Lainey was old enough to make her own decisions, but the old school gentleman in me still felt the need to get her father's permission. I didn't want him thinking either of us were disrespecting him by doing anything underhand. I valued his trust, and I wanted to make sure there were no surprises.

"Sure, he'll be thrilled. But I'm thrilled more," she said, leaning over and kissing me on the cheek. She grabbed her cell phone and called him. As she predicted, he was excited and happy that she had someone to accompany her on her trip. He didn't like the idea of her being alone. Surprisingly, he didn't think our unplanned trip was strange at all and recalled a story to both of us when Lainey put him on speakerphone...

"I remember doing a similar thing with your mom before we were married. She was going to travel to upstate New York for a conference at a big fancy hotel. I couldn't bear the idea of her going alone, and I hated being away from her, so I tagged

along. Well I met her at the hotel with a huge bouquet. She was so surprised, but overjoyed, to see me there. A year later, I bought a ring and proposed at the same hotel. She made me the happiest man alive when she said yes," he said as he recalled the story.

"Ahh, that's so sweet. I remember you telling me that when I was a little girl, Dad. So spontaneous and fun. We have to see if we can get him a ticket first, and if we do, we'll call you when we get to New York," she said.

"Okay, kiddo. Have a good time... and look after my princess, Calvin," he said before he hung up.

And that was it, I was potentially on my way to New York. We parked up at the airport and when we got to the ticket counter, I asked her if she wouldn't mind getting us some coffee. If we were going to do this crazy thing, I wanted it to be a fun surprise. I bought a First-Class ticket for myself and had her ticket upgraded to First Class, as well. I wanted to make the trip as magical and memorable as possible.

I then called the Wythe hotel and booked us a top floor loft with a view of Manhattan and got us reservations at an exclusive restaurant nearby. I hoped it wasn't overkill. I didn't want to come across as showing off, but I was so looking forward to having this short vacation with Lainey. Not only would it be sexy and exciting, but also a great way to get to know her life in the Big Apple a little better. When she returned, I tried to hide the excitement that was surely showing on my face.

"Were you able to get us two seats together?" she asked, handing me my coffee.

"Kinda," I replied. "Best I could get was window and aisle. Same row, though. That ok?"

"Oh... um... yeah, I guess. If that's all they have." She stuck out her bottom lip in a fake pout and looked a little disappointed. "Here's your triple espresso, by the way" she said, handing me the coffee. "What ya planning on doing, cowboy? Staying up all night?" She looked at me with a sexy smirk, her disappointment gone.

"I sure hope so," I grinned back.

We sat and drank our coffee and decided to buy me a suitcase and clothes once we got to New York. I called my overseer and arranged for him to take care of the house and ranch for a week, then I called Lindsay to give her the heads-up that Lainey and I would be out of town.

I asked her to keep an eye on Lainey's dad, which she said she'd already been doing, completely unknown to us. She promised to look after him and said he was a pleasure to talk to and that she really enjoyed his company.

Everything felt great. We were ready for a fun adventure but as soon as our flight started boarding, Lainey became a little concerned when we joined the other First-Class passengers.

"Um, I don't think they've called our row yet, Calvin. Do you want to check the tickets? I thought I was in 16A." She seemed a little nervous as she shuffled into the short line of fliers carrying their Louis Vuitton bags and toy dog breeds in designer soft-sided cages.

"No, we're cool." I flashed her a playful smile.

She threw me the side eye, and I thought I was about to catch lip from her when we started moving down the corridor to our destination and I handed the tickets to the flight attendant.

"Good afternoon, your seats are right here. Seats 1A and 1B," she said as she waved her arm toward the voluminous leather seats that screamed luxury. "An attendant will be with you as soon as the other passengers have boarded," she added.

Lainey's mouth dropped open. She was at a loss for words and I smiled smugly as we walked to our seats at the front of the plane.

"Are you crazy?" she whispered. "These seats have to be like, thousands of dollars each! My ticket was for coach, and I thought you said we had a window and an aisle seat," she hissed, trying not to attract attention. She was a mixture of annoyed and elated.

"Well, we do, don't we? Here we are. You have the window and I have the aisle," I said with a grin. "Don't worry about it, I have the money," I shared coolly as we took our seats.

I could see she was practically on the verge of tears when she said, "I'm sorry. I didn't mean to sound angry or ungrateful or anything. Really, this is the most wonderful surprise, Calvin. Thank you so much. I... I don't know what to say. I've never been in First Class before. This is so much fun," then she took my arm in hers and kissed me.

This was going to be a fantastic trip with Lainey by my side.

Chapter Sixteen

Lainey

The whole day had been completely surreal. First, Calvin agreed to come with me to New York, and then I was sitting in First Class with him sipping champagne. I could hardly believe it was happening. I wished the flight from Texas to New York had been longer so I could bask in the luxury of it all just a little more. It was so exciting sitting among the exquisitely dressed business people and rich passengers and being there with Calvin made it more so.

"So, I guess your farm is doing really well then?" I asked, astounded at how he could afford to pony up for two of the most expensive seats the airline had to offer. On the face of it, he seemed as rugged and hard-working as any other rancher I'd seen. Outside of his incredible good looks, he was what you pictured as a man of modest means.

He laughed somewhat nervously for a moment before answering. "You could say that," he said quietly.

"So, you're not a real cowboy? You're some rich rancher guy who's sticking it to the poor people?" I teased, taking another sip of champagne.

"Oh, hey there, partner. I'm very much a cowboy. Just because I have enough cash to float a trip in First Class, doesn't mean I'm a hoity-toity, snooty patootie." He feigned an expression he thought looked rich and snooty and I couldn't help but laugh at his tirade. Oh my god, he looked so funny.

"A what?" I could barely talk over my laughter.

"A hoity-toity, snootie patootie," he said proudly.

"Where'd you get that from? A country and western song?" I said with a Southern drawl, mocking his accent.

"It's someone who doesn't know how to kick the shit off their boots," he replied, using an even deeper Southern accent than his own.

"So, what are you, a millionaire?" I teased.

"Not a million." I could tell he was being vague.

"Ah, well, someday you'll crack that million, but only if you invest well and stop buying extravagant plane tickets," I advised.

"Who says I haven't cracked it?" His broad smile widened.

"Seriously?" I playfully punched his shoulder, "You lucky skunk!"

He smiled, and we finished our bottle of champagne and watched a movie together. It didn't change things. So, he had money. Great. It didn't make me like him anymore, or any less than I already did. I was already hooked on him before he even told me, and even though it had only been a week, I was pretty sure I was falling in love.

***

We had a connecting flight, so we browsed the Phoenix airport for a while. He found a cowboy hat which made me roll my eyes and cringe at the same time.

"Gotta look the part," he said as he tried it on.

"You already have a hat. Where's the one you wore to the airport?" I asked.

"Oh, that ol' thing? I left it in the truck. That's my working hat. We've been together for, oh, three years now," he smiled.

It reminded me that I'd gotten used to him wearing cowboy hats and they suited him well. He didn't like it, however. It wasn't the $200 price tag that had him frustrated, though. It was the fact that the hat looked too new. God forbid that he should look like a tourist.

"This hat hasn't got any personality. It's just a fraction of what it could be with a little dust, sweat, and grime in it," he frowned.

"Eeeww! That's pretty gross so I'll pretend I didn't hear it, but when we get to our hotel, you can take it around the back and roll in the dirt with it. New York streets are plenty dirty, so it'll be grimy and just how you like it in no time." I gave him a crooked smile.

Actually, I was hoping he'd buy a new one, because the one he usually wore was pretty soiled and had seen better days. We spent about an hour bumming around the airport then we were off to another plane and another set of luxurious First-Class seats. The whole experience was amazing, and we got to New York later that evening and checked into the hotel without a problem.

I'd stayed at the Wythe Hotel once before when a girlfriend and I had a girls' night on the town, but nothing had prepared me for what we walked into this time. My friend and I just got a room with bunk beds and it was pretty cool, like we were kids sharing a bedroom. I knew that wasn't going to work for Calvin and me, but I'd already booked a king room, anyway. He insisted on doing the checking in, which made me suspicious after the last surprises and I let him know it.

"It's my hotel reservation, I get to check in." I pouted.

"Not this time," he winked.

Damn, I knew that man had something up his sleeve and when I walked into the room, I saw exactly what it was. A loft suite at the top of the building with a dining area, floor to ceiling windows with a view of the Williamsburg waterfront, and an upstairs terrace with a view of the world. I was giddy with excitement.

"Oh my god, this is incredible. Wow!" I said like a teenager on crack.

"I thought you'd like it. Luckily, they still had this room available," he said proudly.

"Have you stayed here before?" I was starting to wonder what was going on with this guy. He had an entire life I knew nothing about.

"I haven't stayed here, but a friend has and recommended this room specifically," he said as he walked up the stairs. "Let's check out the loft."

I followed him up the stairs, and While I was so thrilled we were doing this, something started to feel strange about him. I brushed it off, trying not to dwell on the fact that my instincts were screaming at me that he was hiding something, but I was too impressed with the view, the surprises, and the fairytale-like experience to pay much attention to my feelings.

The city looked alive and vibrant below us. It shimmered against the night sky. He came up behind me and wrapped his arms around my waist.

"Do you like it?" he asked softly in my ear.

I looked at him, crossing my eyes and giving him a silly look.

"It's awful," I joked. "Seriously, I'd be an idiot if I didn't."

His arms closed lovingly around me.

"We have reservations downstairs at the Reynard. I'm sure you're hungry," he said as if there might be more on his mind.

"Or?" I encouraged.

"Or, we can order room service and stay here and... um, play if you want." He let his thumb breeze over my nipple as he said it.

Of course, I'd rather stay and play with him. I wanted him all the time. I barely even wanted to talk with him if I could have sex with him instead. I knew that sounded crazy, but I felt like I had years to get to know him and I was young and sexy now—why waste it? Besides, there was something about him. It was if I didn't need to talk to him—he was already in my soul. The rest of my worry and suspicion about what he may be hiding, I put in my back pocket and let lust and wantonness drive me instead.

I turned to him and planted a soft kiss on his lips.

"Of course, I want to stay and play with you," I smiled, kissing him again. "Thank you for all that you've done today. It was so unexpected. No one has ever done anything like that for me before."

I stopped there since I felt like I was going to cry. I'd been so strong for my mom, and I watched her wither and die. Then I'd rallied my dad's dreams together and followed him on an adventure I'd been so reluctant to take. I'd almost given up the on the idea of finding love for myself for many more years, if ever. Family meant more to me at that moment, but here he was, in the middle of nowhere on a journey I wasn't sure I wanted to embark upon. Hidden in the roughness, the dust, and sadness of our loss, was this perfect gem.

He sensed I was close to tears and drew me in closer.

"You're welcome. I'm just glad I could do something for you. Something to make you smile," he said, so caring.

"I always smile," I fought back.

"I know, every day. But I know inside, those smiles are for other people's benefit, not always yours. I wanted to see you smile today. Just for you," he said as he planted a kiss on my forehead.

"You're amazing. You know that, right?" It was a stupid thing to say, but I felt so emotional and overwhelmed.

"No, you are," he countered.

"You sure you don't want to go buy some clothes or anything first?" I asked. I hoped I wasn't being rude by wanting to make love to him instead of any of the activities he'd planned.

"I don't need clothes for what I'm about to do, darlin'." He gave me a devilish smile. "I can always get clothes tomorrow, or we can stay naked all week if you want."

He seemed like an eager little boy. The idea of never getting dressed making him feel naughty and rebellious.

"That wouldn't be the best idea for me. I'm sure my professor would be rather surprised if I walked in asking for an independent study wearing nothing but a smile," I teased.

"Oh yes. No... I mean, no, you need to wear clothes. I'm sure he's fat, old, and ugly, but I couldn't handle the idea of any kind of competition." Suddenly, he was getting all manly on me.

"No worries, Tex. You're the only man for me," and with that, I slid my T-shirt over my head and bared myself to him.

He expertly removed my bra and let his hands smooth over my breasts.

"You know you're incredibly gorgeous, right?" he asked as he let his hands caress my tender flesh.

"I don't always think that of myself, but it's nice to hear it." I thought it was time for some honesty since I was starting to have real and deep feelings for him.

"You're perfect, Lainey. Every part of you," he said as he dipped his head to my nipple and gently sucked and nibbled, making me wild with desire for him.

I responded to him as if he was a virtuoso who knew how to play my body expertly. We were on top of the world, yet suddenly I became a little shy with all the skyscraper windows around us. It seemed we'd already done a fine job of committing a public sex act, but now I wanted to enjoy a little more privacy.

"Can we go downstairs? I want you to ravish me, but I don't want to end up as some voyeur's nightly entertainment."

He laughed. "Of course." He softly took my hand in his and led the way downstairs, closing the sheer curtains across the floor to ceiling windows. Everything about the loft and the night felt so sexy and he lost no time resuming where we'd left off, fondling my sensitive breasts and igniting the fire between my legs. I wanted him to ravage me—every nerve in my being wanted it—but despite my craving, I slowed him down and gave him a long, sensuous kiss. I wanted him to know what I felt for him. I let my hands slide across his stubbled face then leaned in and whispered in his ear.

"I love you," I said as I nibbled at his lobe.

He returned my kisses, pressing his lips hard against my own. He met my passion, lifting me up, and I straddled my legs across his hard erection.

"I love you, too" he proclaimed, gazing into my eyes. "More than you'll ever know." He carried me to the bed and laid me on it then slowly undressed me. I wanted to reach up and return the favor, but he stopped me.

"Nope," he said, "I'm going to make love to *you* tonight. We'll be here all week. Tomorrow, I'm at your mercy, but I want to ravage you like a cowboy in love. I know you're a strong, modern woman, but I'm going to treat you like a princess, tonight," he smiled graciously.

"Um... okay..." was all I could say. I felt so wanted, so desired, lying there naked on the bed in front of him. His sparkling eyes never left mine as I watched him slowly undress in front of me. His stiff cock sprung free, ready for me as it would ever be, and I lay back, spread my legs wide, and gave Calvin a beckoning stare. "I'm all yours, pardner," I said with a giggle.

He lay down beside me and kissed me passionately again while his fingers stroked from the nape of my neck to my belly button, making my body shudder at his touch. He broke the kiss and shifted on top of me, running his tongue along the goose bumps on my neck and sucked hard, giving me what felt like a tiny monkey bite in the place where his mouth had been.

"Hey, I have an interview tomorrow," I warned breathlessly.

"That's just in case the professor isn't old, fat, or ugly," he whispered as he moved downward. "You're mine," he growled.

I giggled as his lips trailed over my body, stopping at my breasts. First, with a soft kiss on each nipple, then a long, sensual tongue massage that bathed each hardened pebble with swirling and sucking, flooding electricity through my body from my head to my toes. I felt my arousal coating my inner thighs as it dripped from my wanton pussy. I didn't want him to rush, but I ached to feel him inside me. I sent him my message by wiggling my hips a little, rubbing my lady parts against his stiff erection.

He raised himself on his knees and gently patted my dripping wet pussy with his hand.

"I'll get there, darlin'," he said as he moved his mouth from my breasts to my belly button. He held my hips as he dipped his tongue in and out of my belly button, simulating what his cock would soon be doing lower down. My needy center ached for him to fill me with his hard, throbbing cock until he was deep inside.

His slow ride down my body continued to my hip bones, and the shaved area where my pubic hair had been neatly trimmed. His tongue swirled around the sensitive skin above my remaining tuft of hair, making me writhe and my breathing hitch. He stroked the tops of my thighs, letting his fingers trickle inward as he spread my legs farther apart. My mind was in raptures—finally, he was getting close to my pleasure zone.

His fingers continued their journey until they reached the outer lips of my sex. They danced upon my flesh, making me squirm then he lowered his mouth to them and lapped in long upward strokes at my wetness. I moaned, breathlessly, as his tongue continued its wild undulations, parting my lips with each upward lick and finishing with a flick on my clit with the tip. I grabbed his hair with both hands and held his head hard against my pussy. I was over the edge—I couldn't hold back anymore. The electricity coiled into knots inside me, and I tightened and shattered with a scream. My legs trembled, and my hips bucked uncontrollably against his mouth, still gently licking and sucking me as I came.

He raised his head and looked at me with a big beaming smile on his face. He looked pretty smug and pleased with himself, and I couldn't deny he had every reason to be after his stunning performance. He crawled up to lay beside me.

"God, that was incredible," I panted, rolling my eyes with the pleasure that still coursed through me. He brought my lips to his, and I tasted a mixture of him and me on his sensuous mouth. I trailed my hand across his body, over the ridges of his strong muscular frame, and around his own peaked nipples as our tongues danced together.

I broke the long, passionate kiss and said, "Just give me one minute."

His face had a funny mixture of curiosity and disappointment on it, but that soon changed back when I playfully slithered down his body and wrapped my warm mouth around his amazing cock. I must have caught him by surprise as he let out a grunt when I teased him with my tongue, moaning loudly in ecstasy as my mouth slid up and down his glorious shaft.

He was so big—I hadn't realized how large his dick was until I tried getting the whole thing in my mouth. No way could I swallow him, so I gave his sweet rod a tongue bath while I gently squeezed and fondled his balls, making him clench with searing desire. I knew he wouldn't be able to take much more, so I let up on him, lapped up the pre-cum from the tip of his cock, then made my way back up to his waiting mouth and kissed him again, straddling his thighs with my own.

"You are one gorgeous sweet woman, Lainey," he whispered breathlessly as I watched his handsome face, his hard shaft nestling against my pussy. I wriggled against him and felt it spreading my wet lips apart and the tip pressed against my aching clit. I moaned against his mouth as I ground against him, wanting him inside me. I moved up a little until I felt his bulbous head nudging at my entrance then he grabbed my ass with both hands, thrust his hips and slipped inside, making me shudder.

With hooded eyes, I pushed myself up and leaned back, grabbing his thighs behind me for support. Now I was in control and I was going to ride this cowboy. His cock towered inside me and with my legs wide, he started a gentle thrusting to meet my

AMANDA HEARTLEY

own as I slid up and down his length. God, the feeling was amazing—his dick hitting my G-spot every time he rocked into me, bringing me closer to orgasm. I closed my eyes and bit my bottom lip then felt a hand caressing my breasts, gently pinching my nipples then another at my pussy, his thumb rubbing my swollen clit. I felt like I was going to burst, then he slowed down, making me crazy with need as the tension balled up in my belly. He smiled, seeing the lustful look in my eyes.

"You like riding cowgirl?" he asked in a deliberately Southern accent.

"Mmmm..." Words had left me—all I could do was moan as his cock plunged deep inside me, rubbing my G-spot with every delicious stroke.

"I'm going to make you come," he growled, speeding up his pace.

"Mmm, mmm... Oh, fuck. Do it, cowboy. Yeah, right there," I groaned.

He made love to me with a fevered passion. I felt his strong thigh muscles tensing beneath my hands as he pumped hard into me. It was too much to bear. I couldn't hold on any longer and I felt my orgasm building then exploding deep within me. My legs spasmed uncontrollably and clenched tight against him as waves of ecstasy rolled through me.

"Oh... My... GOD!" I screamed out as it reached its peak, the warmth traveling up and down my body, and I flopped forward to rest on his manly chest, completely satisfied, but exhausted. He grabbed my ass with both of his huge hands and pulled me hard against him. He kissed me, his body tensing and with one final thrust, he buried his cock so deep inside me. He let out a grunt and came hard, his hips bucking against mine, and I felt his release pooling between us, warm and sticky.

"God, Lainey. That was a helluva ride," he said, smiling and panting breathlessly as he tenderly stroked my back, running his fingers through my hair and kissing my forehead so softly.

"It sure was. I love saddling up with you," I giggled.

This was fun. Having such a good-natured man to play with and to enjoy was such an unexpected surprise after our move to Texas. We pillow-talked and cuddled and kissed in the afterglow of our lovemaking, then showered and went downstairs to the bar where a few hotel guests, slightly worse for alcohol, clung to their drinks.

"What would you like?" he asked.

"Surprise me," I said. He raised one eyebrow inquisitively in response. "You've been amazing with the surprises today," I cooed, still reveling in the pleasure from our incredible sex session.

"Okay, I got an idea," he said as I sat down at one of the tables. He approached the bar and when he returned, he had two whiskeys—one over ice, and one neat.

"What?" I smiled. "Whiskey?"

"This is a cowboy's drink. Some like beer, but it's really all about the whiskey, and this is the good stuff." He smiled like the devil as he handed me the one on the rocks.

"You're not trying to get me drunk, are you? You've already had your way with me," I teased.

"And I'm hoping to again," he said with a beaming smile. "But wasn't it you who had your wicked way with me?" he suggested, tilting his head toward me and raising his eyebrows. "I seem to recall you were on top and calling the shots, right?"

"Calvin, you're the worst," I teased, "but I'm sure you'll get your chance."

"You can rely on it," he said in a low voice then took my hand and kissed it. "Anyway, plenty of time for that. I want to know more about you. Like, what is it you love so much about New York?"

"Um, this hotel, for one," I said, looking around the room at the luxurious interior design and expensive fittings.

"Because of the company?" he asked with a smile.

I cocked my head, raised a finger to my lips and fluttered my eyelashes at him. "Oh, yes. Of course, the company is incredible," I said, playfully. He laughed out loud, causing other customers to turn their heads in our direction.

"Well, I love your sarcastic New York sense of humor," he said. "Do carry on."

"Oh, I don't know. The smells of summer when it's so hot you think you'll fry up and die. Even though it sometimes smells like death, I love all the different foods you can eat and all the different languages you hear as you walk around. Even though you have to squeeze everything you own into a tiny apartment, I still love it. It's nothing like the big, wide-open spaces of Texas. Here you live right on top of one another. Rooftop terraces, fancy cocktails, Broadway, it's just an amazing place to live."

I suddenly became aware I was becoming more animated as I thought of all the things I loved about New York and I'd also noticed Calvin's face drop a little more at the mention of each one. It seemed my enthusiasm for something he wasn't a part of was hurting him, but I couldn't help that I loved it. New York was in my blood, the same way I guessed Texas was in his.

"Sounds nothing like the ranch." He tried to make his observation seem lighthearted, but it was obvious how he felt.

AMANDA HEARTLEY

"Well, it's only been a little while. Maybe the ranch will grow on me," I offered to try to console him.

"Or maybe it won't. I mean, it doesn't have to. You should be where you belong and feel comfortable." He was being reasonable and kind, and I appreciated that.

"The problem is, I really don't know where that is. Of course, I want to go to NYU and study, and it would be amazing to stay here with my friends, but my dad's not here, and he's the only family I have left." I was already missing the old guy.

"People leave their families to go to college all the time," he encouraged.

"Yeah, but he's newly widowed. I'm sure he can hack it all by himself for a while, and he'd never tell me if he started to feel the sting of loneliness, but the evidence of it would be there. He'd forget things

218

and start to meander in life. I saw it happen when my mom was first diagnosed. He just walked around aimlessly most of the time," I confessed.

"That's normal grief, though. That's what it does to you." I knew he was trying to help me let go so I could make my own choices about the future.

"Yeah, it was definitely grief, but I also think he was maybe preparing himself for loneliness. Like he was playing out the 'what if' in his head, and whether he could endure it or not, but I really don't want to test out my theories. He's all I have left, so I should hang with him, even if it means saying goodbye to New York. And then, of course, there's you." Now I was feeling funky and a little guilty for mentioning him last.

"Do you know what I love about New York?" he asked.

"Do you love anything about New York?" I was completely shocked.

"Absolutely. I love that the city never sleeps. I know a great club where we can dance the night away. Are you up for it?" He had a delightfully boyish grin on his face. I sneered at him, in mocking disbelief.

"It's not a line dancing place, is it? Only I don't have my hat and cowgirl boots with me," I giggled.

He beamed a huge white smile back at me.

"I think they've been known to do a fair bit of shit kicking, but not always in a line, God forbid," he said. "This is New York for heaven's sake."

We finished our drinks, and he paid the bill. Even though it was late, he suggested we walk as he said he wanted to make sure I got lots of that Brooklyn air. He said The Bembe club was only about a half-mile away from the hotel, and I was happy to take a walk with him.

It was very late. There were only a few people on the streets with most either hitting the bars, or taking a midnight stroll along the water. It was edgy, yet romantic. I felt warm inside when Calvin took my hand in his and we walked down the sidewalk to the club.

Chapter Seventeen

Calvin

I felt electricity spark between us as I walked with Lainey from the hotel to the dance club. It wasn't far, and it gave us time to take in the late-night scenery. I still felt apprehensive about telling her I'd previously been married. In fact, my ex-wife's place wasn't far from where we were.

We'd spent a lot of time in Brooklyn when we were together. We had a lot of friends all over Manhattan, which she preferred, but I rather enjoyed Brooklyn more so when we got along together, she'd made concessions and—since we were well-known in society—we had several friends in Brooklyn too.

I knew if we had any future together, I'd have to tell Lainey more about my past, but it didn't feel like it was the right time, so I kept all that to myself and was content to hold hands with her and talk about other things until we got to the club.

It was busy outside, but not as packed as it would be on a Friday or Saturday night. The Bembe was a Latin dance club that had great music, sexy dancers, a real vibe, and it pulled the city kid right out of me. There was a small line being managed by a hefty looking bouncer. I approached him, pulled out my wallet, and showed him my former business card. I pressed a twenty into his hand and he dropped the rope and immediately let Lainey and I in.

"Woah," Lainey remarked, amazed that we'd just waltzed to the front of the line. "How'd you do that?"

"I have my ways," I said mysteriously, "The Cosmopolitans they serve here are amazing, by the way. I'll get you one, and I'm going to have a Glenfiddich." I still took the lead, hoping she'd see a different side of me—one that didn't just ride horses and wear a Stetson. By the look of wonder on her face, it looked like she was impressed.

"Sounds good to me... whatever that is. This place is so cool. I've heard about it, but never got down here before," she said, wide-eyed.

"Glenfiddich? It's a 12-year-old single malt whiskey, very smooth. Yeah, I haven't been here in a long time. It's nice to be back. I'm friends with D.R., one of the owners," I threw out, nonchalantly.

D.R. was my ex-wife's friend, but we'd kept in touch after the divorce. I used to travel between Texas and New York a lot, even after I'd left the oil business, but I hadn't gotten out to his place much whenever I'd been in town. Hopefully that would all change. Lainey sparked the need in me to feed that silent part of my soul. The part I'd intentionally left dormant, because it was the part of me I least liked.

I hated the greed, the in-your-face wealth, the power-hungry megalomaniacs who ran this town, and the game I had to play to stay on top. The oil industry was ruthless and cold. It corrupted my wife, but I wasn't going to let it corrupt me. Luckily, I woke up and realized I was treading the same path, so I detached myself from it for years.

Looking back now, I wasn't a nice man. Sure, I was well-known, a man of great power and influence, but I'd become a total asshole. I left all that behind me, hoping to change to something more... normal—whatever that is—but in the wake of my escape from who I was, I also lost a lot of things I'd enjoyed, like dancing at the Bembe. Now, being among all the people dancing to the uplifting beat of the music, that inner part of me—the urbanite I'd ignored—had been re-awakened.

We danced most of the night to the pulsing Latin rhythm. The room was hot, sweaty, and full of eclectic energy. We let our bodies mold together and gyrated to the samba drums, the tempting pulse in the air killing the cowboy in me. Lainey seemed happy, enjoying the music, and boy, could she dance—but there was something behind her eyes that didn't seem quite right. She didn't seem to be the same carefree woman I'd come to love and admire. She seemed suddenly distant.

I wondered if being at the nightclub had sparked her longings for New York and the culture she craved while she'd been squirreled away on a ranch in Texas. Maybe the crushing reality of what she'd left behind was slowly filtering in. The melancholy in her eyes seemed to grow throughout the night and had me concerned. I didn't know what had changed her, so instead of making my own assumptions, I had to ask her.

"Are you tired? Do you want to leave now?" I asked over the loud, heart-thumping music. She looked me deep in the eyes for a moment, then down to the floor. Something was definitely wrong. "Are you okay?" I asked, concerned.

"Yeah, I'd like to go back to the hotel, if that's okay with you," she shouted in my ear over the music.

It was around three in the morning when we started our walk back to the hotel, and Lainey was mostly silent the whole way.

"Did you have fun?" I asked, hoping she'd give me a little hint about what was going on inside of that beautiful mind of hers.

"I did, but I'm really tired," was all she offered back. "Thanks for a lovely evening, though."

"My pleasure." I took her hand, and she held mine for a moment, then broke away. I wanted to stop her right there and confront her on her drastic change in attitude, but I also realized, I may have been getting a little paranoid. Our relationship was still so very new, and she probably was exhausted. We'd started our day early in the morning. It was nearly twenty-four hours later, so I decided to let it go. We walked the rest of the way in silence and we both flopped into bed when we reached the hotel.

***

I'd had a hard time getting to sleep, thinking about what I might have done during the evening to cause Lainey's mood to change so quickly. The next morning, I woke briefly and heard faint sounds, but I was too exhausted to get up. Seemingly, I'd completely abandoned the cowboy who rose at dawn no matter what, and when I did get up around 10 am, the room was still and silent. The blackout curtains were closed, and it felt like a tomb. My heart raced, and I immediately searched for Lainey. At the front door was a note.

"Went to school, see you after. ~L,"

While I quickly realized there was no need for me to panic—of course, Lainey would be with her professor, this was the whole reason for our trip— something still felt off. I showered, dressed, and had a light breakfast of coffee and fruit, and without much else to do, I checked in with my ranch foreman. No problems there, so it was time to buy some clothes.

I went to some of my favorite stores and bought some hip and fun outfits. It felt good to dress in fashionable styles again. I loved my beat-up jeans and T-shirts, but a little switch up felt good. I got back to the hotel with my purchases just as Lainey arrived.

She looked incredible, very collegiate and intelligent. I realized I hadn't seen her in such fashionable clothing either. We both looked like quite the New York couple.... and maybe that was the heart of the problem.

Chapter Eighteen

Lainey

Calvin sat in the lounge, reading something on his phone, and looking quite the GQ model, making my insides twist again. I dreaded approaching him— my stomach was in knots. I'd barely slept most of the night, though he wouldn't have known it. I know he didn't go straight to sleep either, no doubt wondering why I'd acted so strange toward the end of the night.

I'd laid awake and just watched him. I forgave myself for acting rashly and making bad choices, but I was being honest when I made them. I made them with my eyes open. How could Calvin turn out to be so different to the man I thought he was?

That's what went through my mind the entire time I stared at his handsomely rugged face. How could this seemingly honest, kind-hearted man deceive me so completely?

"How did it go with your professor?" he asked, casually.

"Good. He likes the idea. There's mountains of paperwork, but it's probably going to be doable. I have to contact some children's agencies, the school district, and look at some funding sources while I'm out here. I have a lot of work to do. It's probably going to be boring, so I'm okay if you want to head back without me. I might not be as much fun as you'd hoped I would be," I said, alluding to the fact that I wasn't planning on being his toy.

With all the thinking I'd done the night before, the only thing I came up with was that he obviously had some significant past he was unwilling to share with me—and that worried the hell out of me. Sure, we were still getting to know each other, but I didn't want to get involved with a man who maybe had dark secrets. Was he a crook? A player? A serial killer for all I knew? The ease with which he'd befriended me and brought me into his life had me terrified that there was, perhaps, something more sinister about him. Even though it was hard to believe this kind man was anything other than he appeared, there was something wrong about all that was right on this trip.

I kept running over everything in my mind. The flight tickets. How did he know the hotel we were staying in? How did he know the owner of a Latin club in Brooklyn? Why was the flash of a card enough to get us past the line and inside? Why was he sitting in the living room of our suite looking like a GQ model instead of a rough rancher? Why was he so at ease here in New York? None of it made any sense. He didn't make any sense.

"Lainey, it's okay. I know you have a lot to do, I didn't come out here for you to entertain me. You do what you need to, and I'll do other stuff. Let's stay in touch so when you're free, we can be together," he offered.

"I'm just not sure when that's going to be, Calvin. I have a lot of friends to see." I knew I was being cold, but I felt driven to push him away.

"Okay, I thought we might see your friends together, but we don't have to." He hung his head and seemed disappointed.

"I mean, we had fun, but it's not like you're my boyfriend or anything." Too late. My mouth had gotten away from my mind and there, I'd said it. Yep, I'd become a crazy, stone-hearted bitch and now I was sure his head would be spinning. What a difference a day makes.

He took a deep breath and looked me in the eyes. I'd put it out there—me, the one who'd known him all of seven days. Wow, I was off the edge. He seemed calm as he measured his response.

"Is there something going on with you? Did I do something to upset you?" he asked.

"Is there something going on with you, Calvin?" I countered. "If that's your real name."

"What? Oh, I think I get it—" he responded, but I cut him off.

"Who the hell are you? You're this rough and gruff cowboy in Texas and now, in New York, you fly us both out here First Class, you know the hotel, the bouncer at the nightclub... Are you with the mafia? Some sort of organized crime syndicate? Or... or... a drug cartel? Is that really alfalfa you're growing at the ranch, or is it...?" And that's what completely insane sounded like as my mind raced at a hundred miles an hour.

He tried not to laugh, but he couldn't stop himself, and he let it out, uncontrollably. I tried not to laugh too, and I did a pretty good job of it. No mistake, I was pissed off, and mainly with myself for falling for someone I hardly knew. He wasn't who I thought he was, but who was he? Had he ever said? I'd held him up to be my dream guy, and truth be told, he hadn't really done anything wrong. I was just, um... so ready to find bad things, I also saw them in the good.

"I think it's time I confess," he said after his laughter had subsided.

"Oh, God! This needs a confession?" Now I was really freaked. "Please, don't let it be anything bad."

"Well, probably not as bad as you think it is... or maybe it is? I hope not," he said.

"What the hell is it? Tell me." I was shaking and sat down on the end of the couch.

"It's really no big deal, but I had a life here before I moved to the ranch. My grandfather left me the property in Texas, but before that I was co-owner of Ronco Oil, here in the city. I ran the company for several years with my wife."

I just sat and listened in disbelief.

"Your wife? You have a fucking wife?" I was now officially in shock. Nothing made any sense.

"Ex-wife," he corrected. "We divorced a few years ago. We ran the company and had a building in Manhattan. It was her father's company before he signed it over to us. He also had other real estate here where his family was from originally. His sons got the other properties in New York, and his daughter, being the eldest, got the company. She's the overseer now since we sold it to a larger corporation."

"Holy friggin' moly, I can't believe it," I said, bringing my hands to my face.

"I have the proceeds from that sale. I may not look like it, but I'm actually a multi-millionaire."

My jaw dropped, and I felt my eyes widening. "Bullshit. You are so not a millionaire," I said after a few seconds taking it all in. "Are you?"

"Multi-millionaire," he reiterated. "Now listen, Lainey, please. I never meant to deceive you, okay? It's just I hate who I was back then. You wouldn't have liked me. Trust what I'm saying on that, and I've done everything in my power to avoid becoming that kind of man again. What you see now is who I want to be and I'm not going back."

"So, all this... this... what we've done these past days... was it for real, or was I just a welcome distraction?" I asked, hoping deep inside I wouldn't be disappointed by his answer.

"A welcome distraction? You bet you are," he said, smiling, "but please understand, I may have been hasty, but it doesn't change my feelings for you one bit. I'm responsible for the choices I make, and I don't do anything I don't want to do. And you, Lainey, I've wanted to be with you from the moment we first met."

And there it was... so much to digest.

"It just doesn't seem like you, though." I still felt a little crushed that he hadn't told me before.

"It isn't me, at least, not the me I am now. The me I hope I am is a rancher and a sincere lover. The old Calvin was a ruthless, arrogant and greedy son-of-a-bitch, driven only by the pursuit of money. I partied hard and flashed the cash, so I'm well-remembered around here."

"So that's why the bouncer let us straight in at the club." It was all falling into place for me now.

"Yes, but I want to put that reputation behind me and focus on the life I've made for myself." He sighed and gave me a pointed look then added, "There's no denying I'd be really hurt if you left, or decided you didn't want to see me anymore, but I couldn't blame you if you didn't, now you know the truth."

Yes, I had the right to decide, but what would I be deciding? Did I want to be with a man who lied for his own convenience? Or, at the very least, someone who chose to hide some important truths about his past from me. Who was the real Calvin? I still felt overwhelmed.

"It's hard for me to trust people," I confessed.

"I understand. It would be. You've been through a lot." He seemed so genuine and sincere, but then he'd seemed that way the whole time I'd known him.

"I don't know what to say." And that was the truth. Words were not my friend at that moment.

"How about you say, you'll give me a chance? I know I should have told you before, but we were getting along so well, and I didn't want to do or say anything to spoil that. You can end it now if you want, but I think we have something special going on between us. I don't care about money or power anymore. You are all I want, Lainey. So, give us a shot," then he started laughing again.

"What now? You come out with all that and then start laughing?" I was feeling a little exasperated with his light-heartedness at the situation.

"I'm sorry," he said, reaching out for my hand, and I let him take it. "I didn't mean to come across as flippant. I don't mind saying, I'm a little nervous right now since I don't want us to end. That would be a tragedy. It's just that things normally go a little different around here in this city."

"Oh, how so?" I replied, searching his eyes for sincerity.

"Well, I tell you I'm a multi-millionaire, and you want to end it all because you thought I was just a man of modest means. Just a cowboy from small town Texas. Most of the women I know in this town would be wide-eyed and flushed with greed right now. I love that about you... that you don't even care about my wealth," he said genuinely.

He had a point, and I had to admit he hadn't really changed since I'd known him. Ok, so he wasn't exactly what my whacked-out fantasy had made him out to be. I realized then I'd been a little irrational by putting him on that pedestal. I mean, we're both in our twenties. Who doesn't have a past? Aren't people allowed second chances? Did I really care if he had an ex-wife? Did it matter to me that he was once an arrogant asshole?

Nope. I believed him when he said he'd changed and stepped away from all that. He'd been the perfect gentleman since we met, and on the plus side, he loved my hometown of New York as much as I did. He was my oh, so sexy neighbor in Texas. He made me feel like a goddess whenever we made love. *Oh, fuck. Yes, he did!* And he was a millionaire, to boot... A girl can change her mind, right?

"I'm sorry too. I've been judgmental, and it's just... I had a picture in my head of the kind of man you were... and then we came here, and... it just seemed you were a different person to whom I'd imagined. But you aren't different, it's just my understanding of who you are that's changed. I love it that you like New York, and you've been here long enough to know how I feel about it. That's important to me," I said softly.

"Thank God," he said, pulling me close into his muscular chest, wrapping his strong arms around me and hugging me tight. "I was preparing myself for the 'it's not you, it's me' speech for a minute there," he said with a chuckle. "That would have been the worst scenario I could have imagined. I really love you, Lainey."

"I love you too," I whispered, then he took my face in his hands and kissed me so long, so sensuously.

When we finally came up for air, he said, "Listen, I've been thinking. What you're planning to do with the disadvantaged kids is totally amazing, and I want to support you any way I can. You don't have to go any farther for your funding. I'm more than happy to give it to you. It's there if you want it." He smiled graciously.

"Are you serious?" I couldn't believe what was happening. "But you hardly know me. What if you... me... what if we..."

"Shhh. That's not going to happen, ok?" he said with such confidence.

"But, what if—"

"It won't," he interrupted. "You're stuck with me, but to put your mind at rest, I'll have my lawyers draw something up. I never want that to be an issue, and what good is money to me in a bank? I'd never be able to spend it all, anyway." His smile widened. His tone, genuine and proud. "I'd love to be involved with this project. It's an incredible and selfless thing you're doing."

Holy crap. Did I just fall on my feet with this guy, or what?

And that was it. My heart melted for him all over again. We made up, made love, and made the rest of our time in New York so memorable, but both looking forward to returning to Texas.

Funny... looking back just a few short weeks, I'd dreaded leaving my beloved city for a one-horse town in the middle of nowhere, but I'd learned a good lesson to embrace change. You never know what's around the corner.

It was kinda scary to realize that if I'd stayed in New York, I'd never have met and fallen in love with this kind, caring, lovable knight in shining armor, and I was so proud to call him my boyfriend.

He said I was stuck with him. Poor guy. He didn't know what he'd signed up for, but I'd be saddling up on that sexy cowboy, every day.

Happy trails...

THE END

More from Amanda

Irresistible SEAL

A Military Romance

Destiny Undone

A Billionaire Romance

Fueled Obsession

A Bad Boy Romance

Oceans Apart

A British Billionaire Romance

Southern Heat

An Erotic Romance

About The Author

Amanda Heartley is an American author who grew up in Oklahoma. She's writes heartwarming romance featuring strong, sexy men, and feisty, sensual women. Amanda's stories take you on an emotional ride of enduring love and erotic sex that always end with a happily-ever-after and her evocative characters will stay with you long after you've finished the book.

You can join in the fun in Amanda's reader group to talk about love, life, books and hot man-candy.

https://facebook.com/groups/AmandaHeartley

...and to join her newsletter to be the first to hear about new releases, giveaways and free books, sign up here...

http://join.amandaheartley.com

If you enjoyed reading this book, please review it and recommend it to your romance-loving friends!

You can find Amanda here...

www.facebook.com/AuthorAmandaHeartley

www.twitter.com/AmandaHeartley

www.pinterest.com/AmandaHeartley

Or stop by her website at

www.AmandaHeartley.com

Acknowledgements

I'd like to thank all of you, my amazing readers, Facebook fans, newsletter subscribers, beta readers and the most incredible street team for all that you do. I so appreciate your love and support from the bottom of my heart. Y'all rock! And last but not least, thanks to my editor and cover designer who make my words and ideas sparkle!

Made in the USA
Coppell, TX
18 March 2024